HOLM
SWEET
HOLM

HOLM SWEET HOLM

Jessie Lovie Watt

Published by Dr. J. L. Watt,
Hallibrig, Whiteness, Shetland

Published 1994

ISBN 0 9524413 0 6

Printed by The Orcadian Limited, Victoria Street,
Kirkwall Orkney

DEDICATION

This book is dedicated to the late Christopher Angus Jacobson. Uncle Angus was a gentle giving man, full of fun and well endowed with kindness and compassion. He enriched my childhood through his patient hours of fireside story-telling.

Angus was a true connoisseur of people and could relate to those from all walks of life with great tact, sensitivity and abounding humour. He had a talent for elevating the mundane and ordinary things in life so that they became transformed through his imagination and sense of adventure.

He was versatile enough to be a playmate to children and a first class tonic to anybody, old or young, with a failing spirit. I owe Angus a great deal, this dedication is but a token gesture of my gratitude for all the years of support he gave me.

ACKNOWLEDGEMENTS

I acknowledge various forms of support from the
Shetland Arts Trust:

* Invaluable editing assistance from the panel of
readers.

* An inaugural grant of £250.

* An interest-free loan to cover printing costs.

Also I am grateful to the Shetland Enterprise
Company for a marketing grant of £625

CONTENTS

NOTE TO READER

All central characters in this book are fictitious and any similarity to real people, past or present, is purely coincidental. However, for the purposes of setting a realistic scene for the imaginary characters, reference is made to a few authentic local business names of the period, usually through acknowledged quotation of advertisements and press statements.

The places within Shetland and North East Scotland are real, although the detailed address of the fictitious Watt family at number 4, Klondyke Cottages, did not exist. (Records indicate that there were only three Klondyke Cottages, situated near the King Harald Street roundabout). The exact position of the residence of the fictitious Leask family in Whiteness has been kept vague, deliberately, since this particular "big hoose" did not exist. Similarly, Willa Leask's croft has been placed near the Hallibrig Knowe in South Whiteness, a real site, but where no house existed until 1990. This slight distortion of historical topography was thought necessary to prevent any possible conflict with, or insult to, existing occupants of real dwellings. This is particularly relevant in a small community environment.

I have made no attempt to dilute the two distinct kinds of dialect in the book, namely the "Doric" of the Scottie colony and the "Shetlandic" of the indigenous Shetlanders, since I believe that it helps to illustrate the language barrier and the social differences in these two distinct populations of Shetland residents, before there was integration.

Prologue

Crovie is a tiny exposed fishing village on the North East coast of Scotland, established by desperate families that were "removed" from the Highlands in the years following the Jacobite uprisings of 1715/45. A simple church and threescore houses cling like limpets to a narrow ledge at the foot of steep cliffs. The dwellings are huddled close together, gables on to the sea to present least resistance to the severe winter gales. At the time of writing (1994), the village remains largely intact, having withstood the battering of the North Sea for almost three centuries.

On a fine summer day, it is a beautiful, lonely place, a remnant of a past time, undisturbed by modern living. The noise of traffic does not impose upon its unique tranquillity, because the narrow sea wall linking the houses is not wide enough for a single car. The entire village has been designated a conservation area of outstanding national value. Many of the renovated houses are holiday properties and few Crovie residents are descendants of the hardy families that lived there in the last century as an isolated fishing community.

These original people of Crovie, like those of similar villages such as Pennan or Gardenstown, were true fisherfolk. They had no agricultural land and represented a pocket of diversity living a meagre existence on the fringe of a farming hinterland. They did not mix with their agricultural neighbours except to barter haddock and herring for potatoes and eggs. They were a close-knit, God-fearing community, with extreme religious beliefs to match their extreme way of life. They were a race apart, marrying largely within themselves or seeking a spouse from a neighbouring fishing town. Since 90% of the inhabitants of the village had the surname of Watt, nicknames or tee-names were used to distinguish the different families. Sach, Dutchie and Pouffe were three such names.

When winter gales lashed, Crovie was an unwelcoming and desolate place and it was difficult to believe that life

1

persisted inside these bare and basic houses, yet life had evolved there with obstinate determination. People lived, loved and died there. Humour was there, but well hidden by hardship.

Through dedication and hard work, successive generations saw the fishing industry grow in strength. In the mid nineteenth century, Crovie had nine fishing boats of the "fifie" type. This rose rapidly to fifty-four boats by the end of the century, as the fishermen learned to harvest the plentiful fish in the sea. In the well chosen words of Alexander Hepburn:

"The seas abound with fishes, such as killing, lering, codfish small and great; turbbet, scate, mackrell, haddocks, whittings, flooks, seadogs and seacats, herrings, seaths, podlers, gandues, lobsters, partens and several others . . . there is no fishing round the island as we have in our Buthquhan Coast." (1721).

However, the early years of the twentieth century brought an end to these times of plenty. Fish became scarce in local waters and the fishermen around the Moray Firth made an increasingly precarious living. Trawling within a three mile limit of shore was banned by law. Despite this, foreign boats continued to sweep through the fishing grounds, scouring them bare.

By the year 1905, starvation was evident in the village.

———

Today there are no true fishermen left in Crovie and the surname Watt has almost vanished. The descendants of the people who built the village have now colonised other corners of the Earth, the Shetland Islands in particular. Through the eyes of a fictitious family, I attempt to tell their story.

1

The Sea Peasants (1905)

Daylight was fading in the small scullery and it would soon be time to light the lamp. Two women were still bent over the zinc bucket, straining to see the detail of their work in the twilight. A baby cried from a wooden cradle on the scullery floor and the younger of the two women tapped the rocker with her foot, temporarily lulling the bairn into silence. She sang softly as she worked:

"This is the wye the lady rides,
Jumpy smaa, jumpy smaa,
This is the wye the cadger rides,
Creels 'n aa, creels 'n aa."

A small thin girl, Jean, sat up at the bare wooden table, looking at the lamp as if willing it to light itself and wishing the weather would improve. She did not like the driving rain and sea spray that pounded the tiny window and gurgled in through the bottom of the door with a noise like a whistle full of water. The unpredictable wind was a powerful force. Jean thought of it as an important person. She'd seen pictures of Mr North Wind in her grandmother's book: a hazy looking fellow with puffed cheeks, icicles for hair and a gale blowing out of his mouth. He had a voice of his own, roaring in anger, whispering secrets, telling gruesome tales. Today he moaned and sighed, like a restless thing. His restlessness was catching.

As she looked at the source of the noise and wondered about it, the door burst open and her father hurried into the relative warmth, leaning against the door to shut out Mr. Wind. He could not shut out the restlessness.

He took off his leather sea boots and coat and hung them dripping from a hook on the wall. He pulled out a handkerchief and rubbed the raindrops off his face before blowing his nose loudly. Stimulated by the harsh new noises and the sudden influx of ice cold air, the baby started to skirl. The younger woman, Mary, stooped to pick him up.

"Hiv ye finished baiting the lines, lass?"

"I've nearly deen, John, and mither here his only aboot a hunner hooks yet t'bait, but she'll nae be lang noo. I've sheilled aa the mussels for her and I've wupped on a puckle extra tippins far the line wis broken yesterday... but John, d'ye think it's wither t'ging aff?"

"Aye, quine, the win's dyin awa and w'tocht we'd ging aff at the back o' midnight. I hope we've a bittie mair luck t'night."

He looked towards the little girl at the table and held out his arms: "An' foo's my Jeanie?" He scooped the youngster off the chair and sat down with her on his knee. Jean relished the attention and prattled on about the day's events: she'd found nine little misshapen pearls in the mussels that her mother and grandmother were shelling to bait the haddock lines. She had them safely hoarded in an eggcup which she clutched tightly. She proudly held out her tiny hand for him to inspect her treasure, smooth, greyish-cream, glistening pearls, priceless jewels to this young child, if to no-one else.

He looked at them absent-mindedly. "I see, they're bonny."

Despite her tender years, Jean was fully aware that her father listened with only half an ear. His skipper's mind was on other things and his weather eyes were drawn towards the window. Abandoning the useless spoken words, she turned to braille and ran her little fingers over her father's arms. She felt the raised veins on the familiar strong forearms, standing out like tree trunks in the darkness of the little room, tracing out shapes like great rivers on the map of the world. She took hold of his hands. She would know them blindfold: big, rough and scarred, iron clad, with deep cracks in the palms and permanently bent into a crescent shape, mutilated by the daily grind of scratching a living from the ocean. The years of chafing by lines and salt and the numerous hook injuries, that somehow healed against the odds, had taken their toll. Prolonged exposure to intense cold had resulted in permanently swollen fingers. These hands were unmistakable.

John Watt was a good fisherman, working hand lines from an open boat in the winter and a share skipper of a herring drifter for the rest of the year. The larger boat was based at nearby Fraserburgh, "the Broch" as it was called, where there was a better harbour with deeper water. John's crew of four included his two brothers, Dide and Willie.

He was a natural skipper who feared and respected his Lord and the sea. He knew the dangers of his occupation and was aware of the national accident figures with over two thousand men and boys lost in less than ten years. He felt the weight of responsibility for the safety of his crew, the more so since he had lost his third brother in a storm three years ago. Like the rest of his kind, he had developed great strength of character to deal with violent death. There was scarcely a friend or a neighbour who had not lost a man to the sea at one time or another. Yet the sea still ran in his blood and he knew only one other master.

The local fishermen were landing more and more of their catches in northern ports during the summer. A few had moved to the Shetland Islands, lock, stock and barrel, because the winter fishing was better. Shetland was also well established as a base for curing cod, ling, and tusk in the Spring and herring in the summer. Perhaps he should make the migration north as well? It was a big step to take with a wife and family, but they had been close to starvation recently. Hunger gnawed at the stomachs of the Crovie children. Only yesterday he had seen Joe Sach's loonie and the wee Dutchie quine chewing on raw neeps. There was no doubt that the economic opportunities for local fishermen had diminished, proferring no glimmer of a brighter future.

He was jolted into reality by the steaming bowl of fish soup placed before him and he smiled up at Elsie, Mary's mother, as she served up the evening meal. Typical of their winter diet, the soup was lacking in fresh vegetables, being mainly potatoes and dried ling. The potatoes were small and frosted, having been scavenged from a field near New Pitsligo; Elsie knew many of the farmers from her years of selling fish as far afield as Ellon, Tarves and Inverurie. Of course some of the landowners were less accommodating, but James Milne, from New Pitsligo, a reasonable man with thirty head of nowt, did not mind the fisherfolk going over his fields after the tattie picking to gather the leftovers. The soup also had a few of the bait mussels added for flavour. John gently shook his head at the thought that he was reduced to eating bait. He would surely have better luck this night.

Elsie was almost sixty years old but she was wiry and still fit to tramp the farms or take the railway inland, a basket of fish on her back, when there was some to spare. She was known by the inland tinkers as "Mother Elsie" because she often gave them a few smoked haddock or a bundle of old clothes when she could manage. She had a symbiotic relationship with the tinkers, since their camps were well scattered over her tramping route and gave comforting protection to a solitary woman on the roads. It was not unusual for wandering fishwives to be robbed and even raped, though Elsie had not suffered either indignity. However, she had spoken to less fortunate women when huddled around the iron kettle at the crossroads' resting place. Some of the stories made her cringe, especially the tales told by Eli, a Jew who sold bales of cloth. He had stumbled into many horrific incidents in the course of his nomadic experience. He had painted an oral tapestry, richer in the colours of life than any of his gaudy materials.

Elsie more than justified her keep, helping Mary with the elaborate washing and bleaching of clothes, blackleading the stove every Friday. She was the one who made and mended the boat's blankets for the drifter season, taking care to wash them each Spring in the big wooden tub, by pounding them with her sinewy bare feet and then rinsing them in the burn. She also took particular pride in painting John's ballast stones blue to set them apart from the other piles of coloured ballast on the rocky shore. She baked the tastiest fresh bread in a clay flowerpot on a driftwood fire out at the back of the house. The flat breads were separated by plates and layers of little stones inside the pot, a method used in Crovie for generations.

And then, John knew that two women to bait the lines and to help pull the boat up and down the beach was a bonus. Mary was weaker than her mother and had not been so well lately. She suspected that she was with child again although young John was not yet a year old. Jean was approaching six now, a skinny little lass, bright and full of curiosity. There had been a Joseph between Jean and baby John, but he was no more. Always a weak child, the fever had taken him last yuletide, just before young John was born. A better diet might have pulled him through the illness, but the winters here allowed only the survival of the fittest. Although John Watt knew naught of Charles Darwin, he had an ignorant awareness of Darwinism.

Mary looked across the table at her husband's troubled face, silently willing the ripples of tension to disperse. She

6

knew he worried about providing enough to keep them in the winter and she knew he was forced by necessity to go off in this terrible weather but she was unable to imagine any alternative. John had been home since just before Christmas and it was now the middle of March. Soon he would be rigging out the "Elspeth Mary" and setting sail for northern waters. She would see little of him then for several months.

She dreaded the months of waiting and worrying, tuned into the elements and always alert for signs and news of the boats. She did not welcome the thought of this new pregnancy in his absence, but she would not tell him yet; time enough when her belly spoke for itself. Except in matters of the utmost importance, they were a couple who exchanged few words: an action or a glance conveyed all that was needed. There was no room for hollow discussion or voiced discontentment. Spoken words had no power here.

The herring nets were ready in the loft. They had been carefully mended by Elsie and Mary, in preparation for the forthcoming season. John and his brothers had dipped them in the village's communal cutch kettle to preserve the life of the cotton. Mary liked the pungent smell of the cutch. It was also satisfying to finish the annual net maintenance and see the old made new again.

The nets had been harder to mend this year because a shoal of dogfish had snarled and riven them but they had been salvaged once more. Would that life were as straightforward as mending a net, she thought, but the dogfish of life often did more deadly damage. She had tried so hard to mend little Joseph. She diverted her attention towards her daughter.

"Jeanie, if ye've finished yer supper, awa through t'yer bed, quinie. It's nearly eight o'clock already!"

"Aye, mither, a' richt, but can I get a story fae grandma the nicht?"

John laughed at the expertise with which the request was made. " I'll tak her, Mary, and tell her a wee story. I'm awa tae turn in for twa hoors onywye afore ga'n aff, lass. I'll see ye in the mornin."

He picked up the child, who was beaming with unexpected pleasure, and put her on his shoulders.

The optimistic seagulls followed the small boat to shore but they were disappointed. The night's catch was only five undersized haddocks, to be shared between three families.

One persistent gull flew low over the bow, hopeful of maybe a handful of offal. John grabbed its legs, pulled it squawking into the boat and deftly dispatched the scavenger.

"Pewl broth t'morn, lads, an' at'll nae please oor Mary, but I canna mak a better o't."

It was a weary fisherman who walked from the small pier to the house that morning, carrying two little haddocks and a plucked seagull. As he passed the stoney beach, he recalled a vivid boyhood image of the whole shoreline covered with gutted and split salt fish. He had been the tending boy on many a long day, knowing just when to turn the fish over on the warm rocks, expertly analysing their moisture content and frantically rushing to get the cure under cover when it rained. He swung the seagull he was carrying and remembered too how he had once been a dead shot at stoning the would-be seagull thieves. The ghostly echoes of childhood laughter reverberated in his head and he wondered if he would ever see such carefree days of plenty again.

Mary had been up since first light and was waiting for him. He sat down to his porridge and looked earnestly at her. She knew a decision was already made.

"I've spoken to oor Dide and Willie, Mary, and we're takin the drifter up north earlier this year. We're takin the smaa boat as weel, because we've heard tell 'at there's plenty cod aff the west o' Shetland. We'd likely get the chance o' a decent agreement with ane o' the Lerwick firms, Hay & Company or John Brown. I'm telt they'll engage the boats for a hale season and they're offering good prices: 9/9d a hunnerweight for ling and 6/9d for cod and tusk. James Wiseman was up there twa-three 'ear ago and they gied him the hire o' a huttie and a hunnerweight o' coal a week, so I think we maun go afore they've teen on plenty ither boats."

"John, we'll nae manage fae noo till the end o' the summer. The herrin barrel's empty. The oatmeal's near deen and the saat fish is wearin weel awa."

Aye, lass, but some o' the Shetland curers hiv agreed in ither years tae pay the Scotch boats every week, so I would get money sent hame, dinna worry. There's a lot o' the smaa boats selling direct at a market up there as weel nooadays, at fit they caa the Freefield Dock. We'll see fit's the best plan whin we get there... There's even wird o' them biggin a brand new fishmarket in Lerwick, so it must be a go-aheed place, wi mair prospects for fisherfolk."

"Can ye be sure that we'd mak a livin 'ere, John?"

"Aye, quine, thir's nae doobt that it's the top herrin landin port in the hale country noo: A've heard 'at there wis mair than 600,000 crans landit last 'ear, an 'at's some quantity o' fish, lass!... A've hid wirds wi' auld Dodie and he'll look oot fur ye fur a wee whilie till the first pay comes through. I'll see him right." He stood up and headed out the door. Turning back, he added: "Aye, Mary, and dinna be surprised if we come back, syne, for you and Elsie and the bairns. I fear we'll hae tae leave oor hame, lass, so prepare yersel for the worst. We canna wait to hear the greetin bairns wi' empty bellies... You'd better speak to the auld lady, although, kenin her, she likely kens fit's adee better as m'sel."

She did not reply. It was not her place to question a decision that had already worn deep furrows into his brow, yet she trembled within.

The Sabbath dawned fair and flat calm, the sea peaceful, shimmering like glass. The families of Crovie wore their best sober attire and the grey figures walked in a sombre procession to the service for their weekly dose of fire and brimstone. Spoken words had great power here. Some families attended the meeting room that was built beside Number 66, while others walked the mile or so to Gardenstown, through the seaside footpath torn out of the rock, called the "Sneuk". For the brethren of Crovie, the Sabbath was a day of rest and worship. Despite the ideal weather conditions, no Crovie fisherman would dare break this holy day and put to sea.

Jean liked the Sabbath because there were no long hours of physical work and no race against time. Indeed her father had more time for her. As was his custom, that evening, he walked out along the sea wall with her and they spoke of matters of great importance like the Almighty and the sea and the moon and the stars. She knew the stars and liked to be turned upside down to view them. There was the Plough and the Seven Sisters. She could count to seven, but she could never see all seven of them. She marvelled that these bright and beautiful things were here at home in Crovie and yet guided her father far away at sea and he could still see them from distant northern lands. He had told her the world was round, like a ball, so she puzzled why they did not fall off into space and mingle with the stars. She felt so tiny compared to the vast blackness of the sky. She gripped his hand tighter.

9

The silence was intense. She felt charged with the night air and seemed to have heightened senses. She had an queer uncanny awareness that change was imminent. She knew nothing of a sixth sense but felt keenly a kind of inner communication from her father's presence ...and, in the silence, perfect peace.

A shooting star fell. She closed her eyes and wished that she would always feel as safe and secure as she did holding her father's gentle calloused hand. It was one of the rare and magic moments that she would recall with clarity for the rest of her life. No words were spoken. This early recollection would be for herself alone, not to be recounted to anyone else.

The fishermen of Crovie had a post-Sabbath alarm system built into their heads...at one minute past midnight, they suddenly became very active. They made ready to put to sea. Already the wind was up and the swelling sea was gathering motion.

Mary lay awake listening to the ominous sound of the wind. Silently, she enduring the indigestion that plagued her pregnant body, re-swallowing the acrid, semi-digested salt fish that burned her throat. She knew that it would be yet another night of fitful sleep, broken into useless little fragments of prolonged time, each a minor eternity in a slippery, irrational world of wind and worry. She liked to read a little by candle-light, but there were few books. Besides the Good Book, and an illustrated book of children's stories (featuring Mr North Wind), she possessed a prized second or "Edinburgh" edition (April 4, 1787) of "The Poetical Works of Robbie Burns". She opened the volume at a well worn page:

"that hour, o' night's back arch, the key-stane,
That dreary hour he mounts his beast in;
An' sic a night he tak's the road in,
As ne're poor sinner was abroad in.

The wind blew as 'twad blawn its last
The rattlin show'rs rose on the blast;
The speedy gleams the darkness swallow'd
Loud, deep and lang the thunder bellow'd;
That night a child might understand.
The diel had business on his hand."

She muttered a prayer in the darkness: "Dear Lord, look down upon us, Thy children, and let the men be spared and return unharmed once more... I canna hilp being feart at the thought that we'll maybe hiv tae leave oor hame and travel tae the cauld north isles. Lord, gie me the strength to carry oot your biddin..." She concluded silently: "...and if Thou can help me to thole this heartburn, Lord, I'd be much obliged... Amen."

CHAPTER
2
Migration

They had said their goodbyes to the living. Jean could not understand the need to say cheerio to the dead. Nevertheless, she did not dare complain as she accompanied Elsie and Mary to the churchyard. It was a long walk, through the Sneuk to Gardenstown and then up the steep cliff footpath to St John's church at the very top. She was tired by the time they got there and Johnie, bundled in a creel on Elsie's back, was girnin sore and squirmin like a futret to get out.

"Had yer wheest, ye thrawn loonie, ye'll be doon in a wee mintie," Elsie scolded him.

The flowers were laid at graves of relatives Jean did not know and prayers were said. Jean wandered among the headstones, intrigued by the green mossy coverings that some had acquired and the yellow circles of lichen on others. She clambered on the wall and could see the whole of Crovie stretching along the shore, like a tiny crescent of dolls' houses, the pier but a finger out into the ocean. She held tightly to the solidity of the dyke, slipping back behind it, feart of falling off.

Jean noticed that many of the gravestones had hour glasses embossed on them, or eerie symbols like skulls and crossed bones. She wondered if pirates lay beneath the earth there. Folk said that there were real skeletons in the walls of the church, the remains of Viking invaders. She shivered at the thought of all these dead people from the past lying all around her, rotting and full of maggots. She ran back to the safety of the living.

"'Ere ye are, quine, far hiv ye been?" Mary greeted her, "look ye here, noo... 'at's far yer grandfaither lies. John Watt's his name, same as yer dad. Mind you, 'er's five ither John Watts in 'is churchyard, so ye maun mind fit place is granda's."

Jean noted the position with obedient but transient interest.

Jean was not allowed to take her pet rabbit because they told her that there was not enough grass in Shetland. So it was that she carried him up the banks of the Crovie burn, past the farm, and on to the hill of The Law. There, in that wild place, high on top of her world, she let him go in a lonely ceremony. As she looked north, to the very edge of her world, her tears made Collie Head look blurred. She wondered how much further it was to Shetland.

They made the migration north in June, complete with all their worldly possessions, including tables, chairs, beds, the blanket kist, the highly polished brass roozer, a creel full of bonny china, the bedding in rolls, a small box of sepia coloured photographs of the folks at home, a cutting of honeysuckle in a pot from Elsie's yardie and their precious puckle books in a fishbox.

The trip to Shetland in the "Elspeth Mary" was a nightmare for the women and children. Mary and Jean were dreadfully sick during the endless journey. Elsie fared better, vomiting just the once, when they passed through the treacherous stretch of water, called the Roost, south of Sumburgh Head. Their American chiming clock made a terrible racket during that part of the journey and Elsie worried that it might never recover. She nursed the clock, the two children and Mary, who was seven months pregnant.

The small haddock boat was balanced across the deck of the drifter, lashed down and travelling piggy-back style. Jean's childish logic reasoned that they might all be safer inside the little boat, so that if the big one sank, the little one might save them.

3

The Bethel Ship

The young seaman aboard the English smack was little more than a boy, barely whiskered. His smooth naked chest heaved as the sobs shook it. He was full of remorse. His head hurt. His body had been violated.

James West held the youngster, trying to comfort him, talking gently, urging prayer and repentance. The stench in the crew's quarters was overpowering, coming partly from poor hygiene, partly from the barrels of putrifying fish livers, destined to become cod liver oil, and compounded by the aftermath aroma of "chained lightning". The German coper had passed through the fleet two days ago and James West now worked his way among the human casualties in the wake of the grog ship. The young man clung to James, who felt suddenly uneasy with the boy's nakedness and vulnerability.

"Will God forgive me?"

"Ye must pray wi' me for forgiveness...Ye must try to bide clear o' the drink...and the evils that gang wi' it," James replied.

"I will, Mr West...I will!" The boy convulsed and vomited.

At nineteen years of age, James West found great satisfaction in his vocation. He had served two years aboard the Bethel ship, as crewman and missionary. Like the rest of the fleet, the "Queen Alexandra" trawled for a living but was also nurse, doctor, priest and friend to seafarers. Her nets were side by side with the medicine chest and the hymn books. James was proud to be a listener to the sick and lonely, a quiet efficient dresser of the lesser ailments like saltwater boils, and a persuasive voice to wean the weak-willed desperate fellows from the varied evils of a harsh and lonely life at sea. The fleeting system dictated that the English smacks remained at sea for up to two months at a time to maximise their trawling potential. Their catches were transferred at regular intervals to fast cutters destined for shore.

14

James shifted restlessly in his seat, anxious for the briefing to come to an end, keen to be out of the confined space of the captain's cabin. It was the first visit of the Bethel ship to Shetland waters. She was an odd sight with the words "Preach the Word" on one bow, and " Heal the Sick" on the other. James glanced at his pocket watch to confirm the time, which he knew without looking after two years of rigorous routine: 09:00 hours exactly.

"Right then, Mr West, you can proceed ashore," said skipper Farman. "Report back here at 18:00 hours. We sail south again this evening. You are to rendezvous with our seasonal shore agent, Superintendent Miss Little, and prepare a report on her findings . . . and your own observations. We need to assess the need for a permanent Fisherman's Mission presence here."

"Aye, aye, Sir," said James.

"I believe you have family in Shetland?" said the skipper.

"Aye, Sir. My father, mother and two brothers have moved to Lerwick very recently, from Rosehearty. They're fisherfolk, Sir...but, I've never been this far north before."

"I hope you find them well, Mr. West."

"Thank you, Sir," said James, putting his hat on. He looked well in uniform. His deep brown eyes creased into a warm smile on his honest open face as he took a long-limbed stride towards the door and the new frontier of Lerwick. He was anxious to see where his folks had settled.

He fingered the paper with Miss Little's address in his pocket, like a schoolboy. He had always been shy and reserved with women, meeting very few in the course of his work and feeling more comfortable in the company of his fellow seamen. He was relieved to find that Miss Little was a mother figure, somewhat larger than her name implied. A model of efficiency, she greeted James with a friendly handshake and showed him around her modest premises in a town shop.

Miss Little guided James around the lively town, with its overcrowded narrow lanes and main street running parallel to the harbour, pointing out the landmarks as she did so. His family had settled in the North Road, so she offered to take him there. As they walked, he could see that the place fair bustled with activity and she kept up a running commentary of information:

"The herring stations are on both sides of the harbour. The indigenous population is more than doubled at the moment, with over 20,000 incomers employed for the season... I hold open air services most weeks at Gremista, Freefield or Bressay, with an occasional trip to Baltasound or Scalloway. A lot of my work is centred around the fisherfolk who live and work here in the north end of the town."

James stared at the motley assortment of crude habitations extending out the North Road towards a set of Standing Stones. Curing stations also continued to advance northwards.

"Are there nae rules to prevent 'is sprawl?" he asked.

"Well," replied Miss Little, "the yards are considered by some to be a navigation hazard. The Board of Trade monitors the final positions of such works, but they invariably grant permission, such is the need to accommodate this lucrative herring boom."

James's mother was overjoyed to see him. James was shocked at the shabbiness of their new house, but said nothing. He was relieved that his father was at sea since Joseph West had never approved of his son's service aboard the Bethel ship: "Men go to sea to catch fish, James, not to sing Hallelujah!"

Before they left, James had promised faithfully to spend his next leave in Shetland and to consider coming back to join his father.

"I'm sure Miss Little would welcome a bit of help on shore, James?" his mother reasoned.

As they left, Miss Little was nearly knocked off her feet by a barrel hoop hurtling down the road. A barefoot child ran after the gird, cleek in hand.

"Sorry, Missus," said the girl, coming to an abrupt halt at James's feet. Picking up the gird, and tapping it with her stick again, she looked sheepishly at the strangers.

"Fit's yer name, quine?" asked James.

"Jean Watt."

"And far div ye bide, Jean?"

"Ower 'ere," she pointed, " John Watt's my dad. He's skipper o' the Elspeth Mary."

"Aye, I ken him fine...John Sach, fae Crovie," laughed James. "Come awa, Jean, Sha me the wye tae yer hoose?"

Jean liked the laughing mannie and his plump companion.

James was a learned fellow and always wrote well. Based

on his own observations and the Superintendent's vital information, his report was comprehensive:

"Shetland lies 60° N, Britain's most northerly outpost. Barely part of Scotland, acknowledging it even less, the islands have strong Norse connections, having been a dowry gift from Denmark when Princess Margaret married James III of Scotland in 1469. Lerwick is the capital.

The harbour is one of the best natural harbours in Europe, being both deep and sheltered. Bressay Sound can be approached from the south or north-east, the high surrounding landmarks acting as beacons to guide ships to safe anchorage: the Ord; the Bard; the Ward Hill; and the Noup of Noss. Steam capstans have been introduced on many boats so the work of hauling lines is reduced for the men. The harbour is always crowded with a medley of masts: the tall brown sails of herring smacks and luggers; lumbering big Dutch busses lying at anchor; and a kaleidoscope of smaller vessels of various nationalities.

There has been a mass exodus of families from all over the North East of Scotland. The main settlements are outside the town boundary, and the surnames of the migrants have already begun to appear in school registers and census papers: Watt; Wiseman; West; Hepburn; Sales... They have colonised Lerwick's shantytown suburb like ants, many in makeshift dwellings.

The better off have built their own houses in places like the Burgh Road, which is officially outwith the township line. The boundary of the burgh of Lerwick runs from the Ayre of Braewick to the West Dyke at Freefield. The Fisherman's Lodge, a large wooden building at Freefield, is filled with families and single fishermen, while some have settled in Fleet Street, Burgess Street and Pig Street. They have packed in wherever they could find room or lodgings, in washing houses and garrets, and many temporary bothies and huts have been built to hold the migrant workforce. The ground is marshy in the North end of Lerwick, sanitation is virtually non-existent and fish is being cured on their very doorsteps.

Lerwick is not the only colonised site. A similar situation is evident in Scalloway on the west coast and to an even greater extent in Baltasound, where there are streets of wooden houses and place names like "Gamrie Corner". The common denominator of these migrant settlements is that these are all places rich in existing curing stations. There are over fifty herring yards in Baltasound alone.

I conclude that there is an urgent need for a permanent Mission presence in these islands. Furthermore, since my family is resident in the area, I am personally prepared to volunteer as a shore based helper."

CHAPTER

4

The Far Flung Islands (1905)

"Sometimes I tink whin da Loard med da aert,
An he got it aa pitten tagidder,
Fan He still hed a nev-foo a clippings left ower,
Trimmed aff o dis place or da tidder,
An he hadna da hert ta baal dem awa,
For dey lookit dat boannie an rare,
Sae he fashioned da isles fae da ends o da aert,
An med aa-body fin at hame dere.

Dey 'lighted fae aa wye, some jöst for a start,
While some bed tae dell rigs an saa coarn,
An wi sicca great gadderie a fok fae aa ower,
An entirely new language wis boarn.
A language o wirds aften hard tae translate,
An we manna belittle or bö,
For every country is prood o da wye at it spaeks,
An sae we sood be prood a wirs tö."

@ Rhoda Bulter

Jean peered through the door of the butt end room but
quickly slunk into the closet when she saw Elsie
approaching. Elsie pursued her, wagging a finger.

"Harken noo, Jean, bide weel awa ive noo. Tell young
Johnie tae wheesht wi' his girnin or I'll mak his lug dirl!
You'd better tak him next door for a whilie . . . Maggie
West'll gie ye a piece 'n drippin . . . Mind noo Jean, caa canny
wi' her butter if she has ony. It's nae for her ain folk . . . and
dinna dee onything tae nark her noo!"

Mary was now confined ben the house. Her screaming had
gone on all day and Jean had been sent for buckets of water
three times already. The well was a good quarter of a mile
away and she had been scolded for bringing half-empty
buckets . . . "but oh the wind in this godforsaken place . . . 'tis
worse than Crovie . . . 'twould tak a saint to keep that water
fae bla'in oot o' the pail!"

19

Mary stopped screaming in the early hours of the next day and then a quiet sobbing echoed through number 4, Klondyke Cottages. At first light, Elsie carried out a well wrapped bundle. No words were said, but a bitter lump filled Jean's throat, making it difficult to swallow. The "mannie fae the kirkie" came and an eerie half-singing, half-chanting sound spread heartache and sorrow to all who heard it. Next day, Mary rose, ashen faced, to help Elsie bait the lines. Life went on.

Despite it having a residential population of only a few thousand, Lerwick seemed an enormous city to Jean, with so many strangers. Elsie had never seen such a commotion in all her life and worried about the women and children in some of the hovels:

"They're little better than orra shacks of divit and fishbox!" she muttered, ". . . and the bairns are ga'an aroon' wi' their bow leggies an cauld bare docks! . . . Oh me, oh me, it's a sair traughle for some peer folk!"

The "Elspeth Mary" was but one of more than 1500 boats engaged by local firms and curers. Many of the Scotch boats, crewed by John Watt's kinsmen, were also contracted to Shetland curers. Jean recognised some of the names: Grey Skies; Fleacia; Retrieve; Mayflower; Gracie Brown; Violet; Mary Watt; Alexander Watt. It made this foreign place less alien. Yet, the sounds themselves were different, with much more clashing and banging and shouting as these strange people went about their business.

They had been lucky to get into one of the row of Klondyke Cottages and John had pledged much of his share proceeds to ensure this roof over their heads. It was basic, with no sanitation, the nearest toilet being at the point of a nearby pier, the Skibba Dock, discharging its effluent straight into the open sea. Initially, Jean felt quite nervous and insecure relieving herself in this primitive structure, locally called the thunderbox, but she soon got used to it.

There was no doubt that the catches were more plentiful in Shetland waters. Fish preparation and curing facilities were given priority when they arrived. John built a small shed at the back of the house and Jean helped her mother to sand and quicklime the earthen floor to minimise the smell of bait and keep it from pervading the tiny scullery.

Elsie rigged up a simple but effective smokehouse using two large herring barrels raised up on stones, with a metal burning box for wood shavings and two rows of tinter hooks along the top of each barrel. Two dozen fish could be smoked at once and the barrels worked well, covered in damp sackcloth to maintain humidity and slow down the process. The smell was delicious.

On his next visit to Shetland, towards the end of the summer, it was obvious to James West that Shetland had now received a massive injection of North East Scottish blood, straight into a main artery. The fishing nomads had come *en masse*, with their families and their customs and their religion. They had brought their ships and their hardships, and their dry humour. Yet it was clear to James that they were not a homogeneous population, despite their common origins and vocation. James made up his mind to leave the Bethel ship and join his father's crew. Miss Little welcomed his voluntary aid in the worthwhile work of the Mission.

There was so much work of a spiritual and social nature required throughout the winter as well as summer. The extreme life-style of the fisherfolk predisposed to extremes of character: many of the men were eccentric with strange habits, superstitions and religious beliefs; with unusual ways of treating their women and families. Some of them were more competent at domestic duties than their non-seafaring counterparts, taking great pride in such things on and off shore, while others saw a well defined line dividing "women's work" from theirs and would not lift one finger to help with any task in the home.

James maintained a close friendship with John Watt and his growing family. John did not treat Mary like an inferior or a skivvy, but he too observed deeply ingrained family traditions and refused to do women's work. After all, he did have two of them in the house and he always laid his money on the table.

James saw clearly that Mary was the prudent financial manager, using her quiet intelligence to allocate the family resources and to economise where possible. Despite her physical weakness and female gender, she occupied a position of great importance in the family. Thus, James watched as Jean was reared in an almost contradictory household where the female held the purse-strings and was in a sense the boss, yet never questioned being tied to the kitchen sink.

There were extreme views on the consumption of alcohol

in the shantytown. After witnessing the horrors caused by the grog ships, James was relieved that the majority of migrant Scots were teetotal, while only a minority were drunkards. However, on the whole, there was a movement towards the mean as these extreme populations mixed, clashed and partially blended.

Modern steam drifters began to appear, belching out clouds of soot and smoke. The black dust from the coal driven serpents contaminated the outside and the inside of the house and Mary had to choose the days when she hung out washing: if the wind was blowing off the Sound, she frequently complained:

"Ah, me, me . . . tak a lookie at 'is, noo, fair foul wi' soot and grime again!"

John merely laughed at this small hardship and, with a certain pride of involvement in the bustling place, he said:

"Weel, weel, quine, fit div ye expect when 'er's mair than 5000 tons o' steam coal consumed every single week here . . . Awa ye go an' wash it again, syne."

Jean woke to seagulls making a terrible squawking in the early morning and she did not like the smell from the gut factory in Bressay. Always the smell lingered in the air, penetrating the very fabric of their clothes, although her father said:

"It's a godsend tae the fishermen since aa the spare fish can be processed 'ere, preventing the waste of dumping 'em at sea."

It seemed to Jean that the peace and tranquillity of Crovie had been replaced forever by noise and dirt and smell. Compared to the gentle sailing boats, the steam drifters charged through Lerwick harbour at breakneck speeds. Collisions and accidents were commonplace and she heard her father complain of this often.

"They're breaking the law, Mary. The speed limit is fower knots, but yon skippers just ignore it. I feel sorry for the folk trying tae cross fae Bressay, they just tak their life in their hands, ye ken. Still, they're clamping doon on them a wee bittie. A puckle skippers have even been fined £4 apiece this year."

The children adapted to their new environment quickly. It was summertime and the pace of life seemed easier in the longer days. Jean listened with great interest to the variety of strange tongues in this cosmopolitan place, some of which she recognised while others were totally incomprehensible

. . . the local Shetlanders were understandable on the whole, although many words were different.

They went barefoot all season and were made to wash their feet every night before bed, since Mary insisted that "cleanliness is next to godliness". Jean never really understood this tiresome injunction.

One Saturday in August, Mary took her to Goodlad & Coutts for a pair of 3d rivlins to wear to school. She thoroughly enjoyed the adventure to the main street of the town. There were no shops in Crovie and there were so many in Lerwick. The place was alive with colourful characters too. Gideon Pouffe was a familiar face, standing at the foot of King Harald Street, immaculately dressed in a black suit, white starched collar, dark tie and flat, black cap. He frequently adopted this street corner station, preaching his lay sermons to the passers-by in a loud, authoritative voice, warning of imminent hell-fire and damnation.

Gideon was an unconventional fellow, around thirty years old, unmarried, living with his overprotective mother. He was an odd kind of a fisherman, manning his vessel entirely alone whereas similar sized boats operated with four or five of a crew. He was referred to by some as Lerwick's "lone fisherman" and he had been seen to strap himself to the wheel and put to sea in a storm. Gideon worked as a fisherman only when it pleased him. He lived for his Godly beliefs and his vocation was to save the world . . . or at least everyone in Shetland:

"Harken ye sinners to the word of the Lord...Repent and ye shall be saved...Good mornin, Mary,...Jeanie, m'quine." He patted Jean on the head and stroked her shoulders, before fumbling in his pocket for a sweet. He handed Jean a pandrop and a slip of paper with a text written on it. She could not read the text and the pandrop smelt of old man's pockets. She thanked him and squirmed nicely out of his clutches.

"Pay nae heed tae yer cousin Gideon, Jean," Mary said, as they hurried along. ". . . He's a queer lad, but harmless enough".

Near the gate into Fort Charlotte, an Arab had pitched a make-shift stall selling miscellaneous wares of exotic origin: wooden toys, carved animals with jointed legs, lamps and oriental carpets. He was a tall, swarthy man, with a hooked nose and cold, goat-like eyes. His long black cloak and the fez on his head added to his mysterious aura. A monkey was chained to his arm. The animal wore a miniature set of clothes. Never having seen such a creature, Jean asked her mother if it was a strange little child.

There were many other street traders of foreign extraction, some with dark skin, all following the herring workers from port to port, peddling their wares.

Jean was given her usual "dook in the tub" over the weekend and, after suffering the weekly ritual of having her long hair near pulled out by the roots with the dreaded fine-tooth comb, to check for lice, she was pronounced squeaky clean. Thus, on Monday morning, shining and polished, nursing her tenderised scalp, she was enrolled for her first day at the new Infant School in King Harald Street. She looked forward eagerly to her days of learning.

She was amazed at the chatter of so many voices and the clatter of real shoes like gigantic false teeth on the polished floors. The smells of holiday spring-clean beeswax polish and fusty old books were strong in the air. She did not like the screech of the chalk on the blackboard, though, making her teeth dirl. She knew many of the letters already and felt important because she could write out her own name.

The teacher, Mrs Smith, was a stern spinsterish woman who sat for long periods in absolute silence, fingers steepled before her pointed nose, staring clean over the heads of the class as if they were insignificant insects. She had a habit of hitching up her skirts to the knee when seated behind her desk, oblivious to the fact that she revealed her lower legs to the front rows. Her stout legs bore purple marbled patterns on the inside calves, where the blood in her veins had been cooked by fireside squatting. Sometimes she picked inside her ears with a hairpin, although her double standards showed up when she lectured one of her charges for doing likewise:

"Never put foreign objects in your ears, girl... The smallest thing that should be inserted in the ear is the elbow!"

During her first week, at playtime break, Jean overheard an older boy say to another:

"Hey, Geordie, can du smell fish? .. I smell a Scotchie, a dirty Scotchie!"

The two boys then broke into a chorus of: "Scotchie, dirty Scotchie!" Jean was not the meek and mild type. She retaliated by taking the big boy by the hair and swinging him to the ground, where he grazed his knee and started to cry.

"Here comes the teacher, Jean!" somebody called, whereupon Jean hid behind the shelter. After exaggerated explanations by the two boys, she clearly heard the teacher saying:

"Never mind, George dear. It's just one of those rough Watt brats. Best to avoid them if you can."

Thereafter Jean was often the butt of malicious humour and seldom got invited to share in their games. She took to carrying a peashooter with a liberal supply of hard dried peas as a means of self-defence.

During these early days, she chose to sit beside a Shetland girl called Margaret Robertson but later in the term she was shifted to sit beside Mary Wiseman because Margaret's parents had complained about their daughter sharing a desk "with a Scotch girl". Thus school proved to be a bitter disappointment. She was segregated, like others of her name and region, and made to feel like a second rate person. She hated going there. She felt the acute sadness and rejection that so many individuals in so many stigmatised minority groups must have felt since time immemorial. She was not "dirty" and she could not help her origins, but this clear precise knowledge did not make her situation any easier to bear.

Mary Wiseman was the youngest in a family of ten children who lived in Pig Street. Her father was a cooper, her mother a gutter. Mary was a small, undernourished, timid girl, always in trouble at school, through no fault of her own. It was hardly surprising that she was sometimes a bit dirty when all ten of them had to take a bath in the same water in an old zinc bath. Hot water was a scarce commodity: every drop had to be carried and laboriously boiled. It was frequently the youngest child who got dipped and scoured in the dirtiest, lukewarm scummy dregs. Mary was at the end of the hand-me-down clothes line as well.

On several occasions Mary was sent home with a note advising her parents to rid her of lice before sending her back. Lice were a problem in the school, but the native Shetland children showed the same spectrum of clean to dirty. Some of their dwellings were no better either. Jean had seen the filth in some of Lerwick's lanes, with the open sewers and the dung-heaps. There were rat-infested pigsties right next to the shoddy houses at the Slates end of the Burgh Road. It was the pot calling the kettle black, she thought.

Once, after school, Jean found Mary in tears and asked what ailed her.

"Oh, Jeanie . . . Mrs Smith says I have to cut my thumb nail . . ." She held up her little left hand to show Jean the unusually long nail, black underneath.

"I dinna understand, Mary. What's the matter wi ye? . . . It disna hurt tae cut yer nail."

"Weel, Jean, I need m' thumb nail...just like m'daddy . . . it's tae mark the barrels . . . I aye hilp him on a Saturday."

Mary Wiseman was dealt rough justice at the school. Like her brothers and sisters, she was regularly late, branded as a persistent poor attender, having a fearsome catalogue of chores to do at home. In these larger Scottie families, only half of the children went to school on any one day. One of the many determining factors in the winter was boots! Mary's family had five pairs between ten children. It was first come first served. The unlucky ones redded and baited the lines... They frequently got 500 lines as a punishment for skiving yet again. Poor Mary had little confidence when she first entered the classroom and her self respect was soon entirely destroyed by that inflexible institution. By comparison, Jean was stubborn, determined, resilient and she fought to improve her image among those in authority.

She tried hard to fit in but things always seemed to backfire on her, like the day when the teacher asked the class to say a nursery rhyme: they had been told to speak in Queen's English at all times, not Shetland dialect, and the mistress had gone round the pupils in alphabetical order, so that by the time her turn came, many of the well known nursery rhymes had been chanted several times, Jack and Jill . . .; Simple Simon . . .; Humpty Dumpty . . .; Jack Spratt . . .; Little Boy Blue . . .; Old Mother Hubbard . . .; Little Miss Muffet . . .; Little Jack Horner . . .; Mary Mary, Quite Contrary . . . The girl in front of Jean had said:

*"Two little dickie birds, sat upon a wall,
One named Peter and one named Paul.."*

Jean had the names Peter and Paul fresh in her mind and desperately wanted to please by coming up with another rhyme. She heard herself say:

*"Peter said to Paul, my dock's cauld,
And Paul said to Peter, weel, heat it wi a heater!"*

26

There was a long silence, eventually broken by sniggers from the back. Then the teacher made an exaggerated gasping noise like a bicycle tyre with a puncture. She shouted:

"Jean Watt! That is NOT a nursery rhyme. I have a good mind to wash your foul Scotch tongue with soap and water. Go and stand in the corner, facing the wall!"

She got to know every blemish and scratch on that corner before very long and she would refuse to drink her tea at home in the mornings, just in case she was made to stand there with the added discomfort of a full bladder and no possible chance of relief.

When the books were distributed, again she was always at the end of the alphabetical order and usually received the tattiest, raggiest copies, with missing pages. The problem was self perpetuating because, on handing them back after use, she was frequently lectured on the need to look after school texts, while Mrs Smith made "Tut! Tut!" noises and flicked over the loose pages disapprovingly. The pristine books were given to those whose surnames conveniently fell between A and V.

She went home in tears many times that first year. It was towards its end that she asked her mother:

"Mam, can we nae change oor name tae something else? I dinna like being a Watt."

This request was often made during her early years at the Infant School.

She yearned for the weekends. Sometimes, as a very special treat, John took the whole family aboard the "Elspeth Mary" and they sailed round to the back of Bressay, anchoring off the beach at Beosetter. The women and children were then expertly ferried ashore in a small rowing boat. The white sandy beach was lovely. They swam in the crystal clear water, giggling and splashing to mask the shock of the cold. Elsie collected whelks, Mary lit a camp fire and cooked them in a can. They all picked the flesh out of the shells with a bent pin and ate their fill. Such family outings were too few . . . and always over too soon.

Later, when Jean graduated to the Central School and got elementary cooking lessons, she and a few of the older girls gave away their practice produce to feed the younger Scottie children. It touched the heart to see the skinny urchins queuing on the landing to receive food hand-outs. The world was not a fair place.

When she was twelve years old, she won a prize for being top of her arithmetic class. She was bristling with pride and keen to have her parents attend the small prizegiving ceremony. Mary flatly refused to come, claiming that she had no suitable clothes. Her father said that he might come along if he was not at sea. On the day, John Watt did come to the gathering, arriving at the last minute. Jean spotted him standing quietly at the back of the hall, cap in hand, pride in his face as her name was called out. He did not hang around to mingle with the other proud fathers or the ladies with their Sunday hats skewered to their coiffured heads with hatpins. He left early, without any fuss. Later, at home, he patted Jean on the head:

"Weel done, quine! I wis' ere. . . but there wisna mony o' my kind . . . I winna be back tae the likes o' yon, but I'm right prood o' m'quinie . . . You're as good as them 'at thinks they're better. Never forget that, lassie."

By the time she had served her eight years at school, she was fully confirmed in her awareness of the uneven justice of the world. She was also held firmly in her social class by the ghetto mentality. She was bright, she longed for further education as a ticket to freedom, but the inflexible education system did not allow scope for redress of its own shortcomings and made little attempt to restore the battered confidence of the Scottie fisher families. There was an ingrained force of mutual antipathy between the two.

Seven of Jean's classmates died during those years, two of bronchitis, one of whooping cough, one of measles, one of scarlet fever and two of tuberculosis. She was strong on a good wholesome diet of fish and she survived. Mary Wiseman did not.

5

Herringopolis

*"The wetness of the ground in the yards, right up to
the huts is made offensive by the tramping into it of
herring and all sorts of refuse . . . the majority of the
farlins stand uncovered . . . the covers where they have
been provided are primarily for the protection of the
herring from sun or rain; for the workers they are of
very little use . . . strong and vigorous as these women
are, they are by no means proof against rheumatism
from which many of them suffer greatly, and while
their scattered homes make it impossible to connect
definitely this employment with any special death rate,
there are two districts from which large numbers of
fishgirls come – Lewis and Shetland. In these, the
phthisis (TB related) death rate is a high one. In the
town of Lerwick, the conditions are worse, if there can
be any comparison drawn at all, because all around is
a thickly populated district and the absence of any
efficient means of scavenging (refuse collection) causes
a continual menace to health. Many of the yards have
no sanitary conditions at all for women."*

*(Extract from the Lady Inspectors to the Factories
and Workshops annual report)*

James West enjoyed his part-time Mission work in
Lerwick. Following two visits by the Mission's honorary
chaplain, the Rev. C. H. Hicks, in 1910 and 1911, aboard the
Bethel ship "Ashton", the need for a permanent branch of the
Royal National Mission for Deep Sea Fishermen was at last
acknowledged. Thus, in 1912, a small building at Garthspool
was rented and skipper Harry Westcott was put in charge of
the shore work. James continued to help on a voluntary
basis. Then, in late 1912, the Tolbooth was rented and the
Mission activity moved from Garthspool.

Throughout these years, when not at sea with his father,
James spent much time in study, reading books, faithfully

keeping a record of events. Extracts from his diary told much about the times:

"May 30 1913. The herring season has recently opened in the Western Isles, with the immature "matties" which will quickly develop into mature fish as they migrate north. The Orkney/Shetland season will last through June and July, and then the shoals usually move down the north east coast during late summer, reaching the coast of East Anglia in October. The English season normally lasts till after Christmas, before the winter migration continues round the coast of Britain, through the Irish Sea, ending up off the coast of Northern Ireland in April. April is always the quietest month.

June 10 1913. The hustle and bustle in Lerwick has increased to a frantic pace, with the building of piers and huts continuing to alter the topography of the north end of the sprawling town. The demands for seasonal labour has again swamped up all the locals and caused an increase in the imported workforce. Lerwick has overtaken Baltasound as the "Herringopolis of the world" with over forty curing stations distributed between the Lerwick and Bressay sides of the harbour. Herring rules these islands without a doubt.

The temporary workers come from all parts of the mainland, following the "silver darlings". In addition to the Scottish and Irish staffing the yards, a cosmopolitan effervescence has again enlivened Lerwick: Germans, Norwegians and Swedes are frequently seen in the Mission. The clogs, peppermints and red neckerchiefs are the distinctive hallmarks of the Dutchmen. The Dutch are present in great numbers and can be seen coming and going from their established social centre, the Albert Hall at Freefield. The Mission maintains strong links with this organisation.

June 12 1913. The town buzzes with errand boy bees: young lads employed by local merchants to keep a constant vigil on new vessels arriving in an attempt to be first to secure custom in a very competitive market. The English boats are like honey to these bees since they seldom make a trip home during an entire season and their continued orders over several months are highly valued. There is always a mad scramble as these "runners" or "catchers" try to be first in the wheelhouse of a new arrival, to solicit the skipper. Sometimes the crew have a favourite bee from the previous summer, and will dismissively clip any other eager competitors round the earhole when they come aboard.

June 15 1913. *This is a restless year in many ways. The industry is enormous and growing fast and furious. There are fears of capitalist take-over as the poverty of the workers and the prosperity of the merchants become evident. Many curers now live in grand houses; the higher income groups having climbed the social ladder to settle the impressive new villas in St. Olaf Street and King Harald Street. In stark contrast, the coopers and yard staff live on the breadline, finding it difficult to feed their families during the winter. The Mission tries hard to give moral and spiritual support to our people (although sometimes I suspect that financial support would do more for them.) The non-unionised gutters and packers are ruthlessly exploited by some of the curers. A few are fairer than others, but the vast majority are flagrantly out to line their own pockets. It is difficult to strike or take individual action against the poor pay and squalid conditions.*

June 21 1913. *There is little doubt left in my mind that the host town of Lerwick has rejected the Scottish shantytown graft. It has been treated as a parasitic mould, growing where it is not wanted. As is typical of human nature, the children at school are one of the main vehicles of expressing the prejudice, yet they merely reveal and broadcast this deep-rooted bias from their parental homes. The Scotties are treated like lepers and, being proud people, they have largely withdrawn into their outcast community. There is much work for the Mission to do here. Despite Shetland's long history of fishing, it appears to have been a part time occupation, going hand in hand with subsistence crofting in the rural areas. Lerwick itself scarcely had any full-time fishermen before the arrival of the Scottie colony.*

These fishing families have great pride of blood and ancestry and are entirely self-reliant. Salt water runs in their veins, giving them an innate sense of their calling and their history. The noble pride and defiance of countless generations shines in their faces. They have respect for learning but not for riches: they will gladly doff their caps to a doctor, teacher or minister, but seldom to the rich or noble. They cannot be robbed of their independence. I am proud to be one of them. Many of the larger families simply cannot manage to make ends meet, despite chaving from morning till night. As has long been customary in large fishing families in the North East of Scotland, some of the older children are put to live with smaller families as unpaid helpers. I am happy to advise on such placements. At the very least this allows them to have

31

enough to eat, although it is often misconstrued by the indigenous Shetlanders as a callous act of "giving a child away".

June 24 1913. *Today is a traditional festival for the Dutch . . .*

Jean firmly believed that the Dutch celebrated her father's birthday, which happened to coincide with the feast of St. John. They did not go fishing until after that date, although they gathered in preparation some weeks before, like an excited flock of geese prior to imminent migration.

The Scottie community had many characters. Gideon Pouffe had grown more eccentric with age: he continued to air his testament on street corners and to promote his extreme form of religion at every opportunity. He paid regular home visits to all his relatives, leaving texts, saying a prayer for the household, fussing over the children. Jean did not like Gideon, despite his gifts of sweets...he was too tactile and never looked her in the eye. Another notable character was Teenie's Black Jock, a slightly built, fiery tempered fellow, a little short on the finer points of personal hygiene, as the nickname implied.

Jock was preyed upon by Lerwick's teenage hooligans, idle boys with nothing better to do than to poke fun at him, shouting abuse like "Old Jock, Black Dock.." and worse, until his temper flared and he chased them with a stick. He was nevertheless a likable character, at his most vulnerable when he was intoxicated. He liked his dram, and he drank to forget some bitter past experience, so people said. The elbows of his jacket were always ragged. In the winter he wore an outsize greatcoat with unmentionable foodstuffs in every pocket, the knees and seat of his black twill trousers were shining with grease and his skin had acquired a distinctive black ingraining that came from years without recourse to soap and water. He looked a bit like a tortoise. It was rumoured that a good scrub would kill old Jock. The teasing youths sent him a present of a bar of carbolic soap at Christmas.

Yet, beneath his grimy, eccentric facade, Teenie's Black Jock was no fool. He was a carpenter by trade and did first class jobs when he put his mind to it. He played the mouth-organ and could pluck a tune from several other musical instruments. He made up the lyrics of songs to suit the occasion and was frequently a carefree jolly person, always willing to pass the time of day with his friends and well liked

32

by the regular docks clientele. He dossed in an upturned boat near Hay's dock. The boys would play tricks on him in the early morning. They would shovel up a fresh pile of dog shit, wrap it in a few layers of old newspaper and set light to the paper outside Jock's boat. Then they would knock, shouting "Fire! Fire!" and scramble off to a safe distance. Jock would run out and stamp furiously on the burning papers, leaving him with even more unsavoury feet than before.

He took a fancy to Elsie soon after the family arrived in Shetland. Mother Elsie regarded him as little different from her tinker friends back in Buchan. He got short shrift from her unless he spruced himself up, but he still spent many an hour in her company, doing odd jobs in return for the occasional meal. They argued constantly. Many a time he was seen leaving the yard, cap in hand, stroking his newly washed spaghetti whiskers and muttering to himself:

"Jock, dee this! . . . Jock, dee that! . . . Jock, tak a bath! . . . and then, fit div I get? . . . nothin fur ma supper but tongue and cold shoulder! . . . Tongue and cold shoulder! . . . 'At's women fur ye!"

Jock made good rivlins and he was a kind hearted man. On several occasions, when he encountered someone who seemed worse off than himself, he took the rivlins off his feet and handed them over without comment. Then he walked home in his socks to make himself another pair.

Jean was 14 years old, barely into puberty and, like many of the young females, driven by necessity and lured by the promise of money to spend her first season at the herring. Once she realised that there was no chance of a scholarship, she did not regret leaving school to join the gutting. School had been a traumatic and degrading experience. She had learned that she carried the stigma of being a "Scottie Watt". She was set apart, not by colour, but by ancestry.

She had stopped wishing that she could change her name. She was developing an inner strength of character. She valued honesty and respected the hard work she saw in her parents. She had great confidence in her own intelligence. She knew that she had an able mind and would continue to learn from the school of life. She eagerly gleaned knowledge from all sources. She detested but failed to understand the class distinction practised by so many of these clannish islanders.

She accepted her first arles of £1 (acceptance of this earnest money signified an unwritten but binding agreement) in the Spring of 1913. She joined two older Scottish women to make a typical crew of three, two gutters and a packer. Babs, aged 19, was a gutter and her mother, Nellie Wiseman, the packer. Mother and daughter were an experienced pair, having worked through several herring seasons. In previous years, Annie, Babs' older sister complemented the crew as the second gutter but she had now married a cooper and was big with her first child. It was with some reluctance that Nellie agreed to take on Jean as a replacement. It would slow them down to have a young untrained lassie although she seemed keen enough and John Watt had asked her as a favour.

Nellie and Babs were not permanent residents of Shetland. They came from Fraserburgh and followed the herring from port to port. Nellie's husband had been lost at sea several years previously and they had fended for themselves ever since. Like many of the migrant workforce, the Wisemans shared a hut at Gremista and Jean spent much of her time there. It was crowded now at home, with her brothers John and David and new sister, Jessie. Another child had arrived every second year since they had settled in Shetland.

Overcrowding was everywhere, the fisherfolk packed as tight as the layers of herring in a barrel. Jean read in the Shetland Times that a Royal Commission report had produced massive documented evidence on the deplorable conditions in the North Road shantytown. Dr. Yule, the medical officer, had certified nineteen houses in the area as "unfit for human habitation". Jean knew that if a family was evicted, the Poor House was the only alternative because of the lack of basic housing. By moving into the hut with the Wisemans, she eased the situation at home a little.

The landing of the herring dictated the working hours of the crew. Following a good landing, they worked from 6 a.m. to 10 p.m. Every morning, shortly after five o'clock, the quietness was violated by the shrieking voice of a cooper:

"Up and tie yer fingers, lasses!" The greeting was followed sometimes by an unwelcome addendum: "Look oot for torn bellies the day!" This indicated that the herring were in a substandard soft condition, their bellies having been torn by scavenging fish while still in the net. The girls' fingers were inclined to go through the flesh during handling. It was also known for some dishonest curers to tear the bellies of fish deliberately during a pre-purchase inspection of the catch.

This they did by using a metal spike attached to an ordinary looking ring on their finger. The fish were damaged when the spiked hand was run through them so decreasing their market value.

Jean learned how to prepare washed flour bags to make bandages. Then the points of the fingers were bound with these "cloots" to shield them against the salt and the knives and they were kept on all day. She had to wash her hands before meals with them on and still her skin grew sore and hacked.

The hut was basic and sparsely furnished with two bunk beds along the wall and a table. Many of the neighbouring women slept three to a bunk, two crews sharing a single hut, but Nellie Wiseman was a long-standing and respected worker and had been given the luxury of a hut for the exclusive use of her crew. A "glory hole" had been curtained off in the corner for toilet use, and there was running water in the form of a single outside tap, serving all the huts. Jean and Babs clubbed their meagre resources to buy four rolls of wallpaper to brighten the place up. Nellie chastised them for what she called a needless waste of money, but they did not grudge spending the 8d from their arles.

Babs and Jean slept in the top bunk, giving the old lady the privilege of the lower bed for herself. Jean quickly learned that Nellie's word was law and she was not to be crossed. She was a disciplinarian who did not tolerate slackers or weaklings. That summer, Jean's education really began: she saw great loyalty among the working crews; she experienced work that was totally exhausting and yet fulfilling; and she accumulated a vivid vocabulary of swear words from certain workers whenever their best laid plans went agley.

Singing was a popular activity on the yard. It was used to mask anxiety and to break the monotony of the daily grind. They sang to lift their failing spirits at the end of long tiring shifts, mostly Sankey hymns. Many tongues participated, Irish and Gaelic being commonplace. Jean enjoyed the strangely moving experience of being involved in this impromptu choir, especially on a calm summer's night with not a ripple on the harbour. A few women would start to sing "The Old Wooden Cross" and soon the whole workforce of their yard joined in. Then the same tune was picked up by gutters at neighbouring premises. It rolled on and on like a slow symphonic movement through the dozens of stations on both sides of Bressay Sound. What began as a gentle chorus grew and swelled into a rich tidal crescendo involving thousands of united voices. Many of the congregation had tears in their eyes.

As they sang, they were blissfully unaware that the threat of World War grumbled along in the background.

6

Pride, Prejudice and Premonition

There were several other girls aged fourteen working at the herring and Jean made many friends. The inferiority she had felt at school lessened in intensity, although not in essence. It remained deep rooted. She was among her own kind even although many Shetland girls worked alongside her, from places as far afield as the isles of Whalsay and Burra. They were united in spirit. With the exception of some good-natured rivalry about workspeed, they were all equals at the gutting. They "kemped", or competed, with each other. Respect went to the crew who turned out the most barrels. Because of Jean's inexperience, the Wiseman crew lagged well behind in the first part of the summer and Nellie never ceased yelling:

"A'm nae ga'n tae carry you on ma back noo, Jean. So get a bloody move on wi' yer gypper".

Before the end of the first month the Wiseman crew had increased in speed and were upranked in status, although they were never top crew that year. Jean was pulling her weight with all the skill and speed of an older hand. She was young and nimble fingered. Nellie Wiseman was a good tutor, who moulded the malleable virgin worker into her particular way of doing things. Jean hated it when she was called upon to help unload the salt boats. It was backbreaking work to roll the dirty two and a half hundredweight barrels of salt from the deck to the quay. Some days were quieter, of course, but there was always filling up (topping up the barrels that had settled from the day before) or cleaning to do.

Buyers came from foreign places like Russia to inspect the herring and lids were taken off the barrels at random. They were all numbered and if such an inspection revealed badly gutted or packed fish, the coopers could pin-point the culprit crew and exact loud and long retribution.

The weekend saw the return of many of the boats. It was the time when husbands and sweethearts met up with their women. The huts were a joyful place to be on a Saturday night with music and singing and plenty to eat. Jean saw the joys and evils of drink from a spectator's point of view. There was much good-natured laughter and numerous harmless practical jokes as well as the odd malicious one, like the night Jean witnessed the mock marriage of an unfortunate idiot boy to a notorious elderly whore. The lad, a good looking simpleton, unburdened by personality or intelligence, was full of whisky. He underwent the ceremony in all seriousness and truly believed himself to be married to the woman by a man of the cloth. He was devastated when the truth was revealed to him the following morning and was consumed by guilt for weeks afterwards over what he saw as his mortal sin. He had also given all his worldly pounds and pennies to his wedded wife and never saw them again.

It was on another lively Saturday night that Jean lay in a fitful slumber in the hut. Unusually, she was alone since Babs and Nellie were visiting a neighbour where a birthday celebration was in full swing. Jean had left the party early. She was exhausted, her whole body ached and her right index finger had gone septic, caused by a herring bone under the nail. She had removed the bone with her teeth earlier in the week, but the poison had set in and it was now swollen and throbbing badly. Such injuries were less common in the older women, who seemed to know the best precautions and cures. Jean had never experienced anything so excruciatingly painful but she was loath to complain for fear of being thought a slacker. She was fevered and slept restlessly. It was then she had a strange dream she was to remember ever after.

The dream was vivid. *It was cold and the biting Shetland wind whirled strong and cyclonic. Hail stung like needles. Her blonde hair was blowing in all directions and she was struggling through deep heather with a heavy creel of herring on her back. It was dark and she strove to reach the light of a house in the distance. It seemed to symbolise warmth and shelter and safety. It was a strange place and she sensed danger lurking nearby. At last, she reached the light and touched the handle of the door. The dream was so graphic that she could feel the cold hard metallic latch in her hand and her sore finger throbbed. The door opened with a bang. Inside she saw a stranger, a man with disturbing, soul-piercing eyes. He brandished a blade, which she recognised as her own filleting knife, and it was covered in blood. She felt trapped, too tired to retreat. When the man beckoned, she had no power to resist. She heard the click of the sneck behind her . . .*

Then she saw the reason for the stained knife: a sheep had been slaughtered and it hung by the hind legs from a hook in the rafters. The throat was cut and scarlet fluid dripped into a pail on the floor. The man uttered no words but held out his hand and Jean instinctively knew she had to give him the creel. He skilfully gutted all the herring into the bucket, so that the offal mingled with the sheep's blood. It curdled and a rancid unsavoury smell arose from the cocktail. A writhing mass of maggots appeared. She felt a sick rumble in her bowels.

She woke with a start. She was soaking wet with sweat and her menstrual blood had saturated her underclothing.

She became aware of a presence in the hut, a moaning and rustling noise. She froze, too scared to move, brittle with fear. This was not the dream, but stark reality. There was someone else . . .

The room was not entirely dark and she strained hard with her eyes in the twilight until they locked on the undulating silhouette of two lovers. They were lying on the floor, partially undressed. She did not recognise them and they were unaware of her vigil. She was mesmerised and could not look away. She could not see the detail of their secret embrace but the passion and the lustful urgency emanating from their union made her own body ache. She felt ashamed of this peculiar new sensation and very guilty. She was relieved when they left as silently as they they had entered.

Nellie and Babs returned to find her in tears, frantically washing her underclothes and nursing her hand. She must have looked as miserable as she felt.

"I'm sorry, Nellie," she sobbed. " The chaff-seck's markit . . . I couldna hilp it."

"Never mind 'at, quinie," Nellie said, patting her gently on the shoulder. " Let's have a lookie at that hand?"

She carefully scrutinised the poisoned finger. "Weel, we'll have tae lance it, quine. It's beilin. Babs, bile a kettle o'water and clean up my knife."

Babs held Jean's hand down and Nellie slit the inside pad of the offending finger with a single precise cut. Jean barely felt the wound and watched surprised as the pus oozed out and eased instantly the pressure and pain. Her hand was held downwards and gently squeezed from the wrist, with a sort of pumping action. Then it was steeped in bleach and hot water to complete a primitive but effective first-aid. Clean cloots were tied on and Jean sobbed with wonder and pure gratitude. She slept late next day.

On the Sabbath morning the girls attended the meeting room in Gremista and the service was joyful with hymn singing. James West lifted his hat to them and smiled. Jean thought of the quiet, smiling Mission mannie as she walked to Klondyke cottages. She went home every Sunday afternoon to visit her family and she regaled them with lively accounts of the week's events, recounting every, or nearly every, new experience.

She spoke of the strange dream to her grandmother. Elsie was considered by many to "hae the gift" and spoke sometimes of future events, both good and bad. She was the family soothsayer and would often rise in the early morning and speak of the "Elspeth Mary surrounded by pewls" and "low in the water" to forecast a good catch. She had foretold the sea disaster in Crovie in 1902, when her eldest son was lost. Elsie listened intently and then said:

"Weel, m' quine, the mixing o' fish and sheep's bleed wi' sic a queer ootcome, I dinna like ava! I believe it's a warning to bide clear o' them that works this land. Efter aa, Jean, we ken ony too weel that the corn and the cod dinna mix. Caa canny, lassie...ye maun mak yer bed among yer ain kind."

Jean had no intention of doing otherwise.

By Monday morning, her finger was much better. However, Nellie insisted on her paying a visit to the finger dresser at the fish-girls' rest-hut at Holmsgarth. It was run by the Committee on Christian Life and Work of the Church of Scotland. Jean became a regular client that first summer, suffering numerous minor injuries when the razor sharp filleting knife overshot its target, usually towards the end of a long day when she was limp with fatigue. The dressers were a great help in nursing the raw open wounds and they were experts at removing small bones. She specially liked it when James West occasionally dressed a wound for her at the Mission. He too looked forward to her rare visits, always recording them, along with other important events:

*"**September 5 1913.** I have noticed a slight dip this year in the peak of the herring boom, which seems to be consistent throughout the UK, but it is not a reduction of great consequence, since almost three million barrels have already been exported to Europe this season by northern curers.*

Today, while on duty at the Mission's first aid post, I met Jean Watt again. She is grown to be a fine lass."

By the time they made the trip to Yarmouth in October, Jean's hands were embryo versions of her father's, well seasoned and, thankfully, prone to fewer accidents.

She returned home for Christmas, glad to be out of the bone gnawing cold of the Yarmouth open curing yards but sorry to say goodbye to Babs and Nellie. They had become like her own family.

She had her own money for the first time in her life, having earned the respectable sum of £12 6s 9d for her season's work and she had bought presents for everybody. She was bristling with pride when she handed the gifts over to Johnie, David and little Jessie. Johnie was delighted with his penknife, and she gave colourful spinning-tops to the little ones. A stick of Yarmouth rock satisfied her father's sweet tooth. She had procured a new teapot for her mother and a fancy pinnie for Elsie: black with little red and yellow flowers on it. The teapot and the pinnie were displayed for visitors and given pride of place.

The scullery buzzed with the happy hum of two competing spinning-tops and little Johnie carved his name on the lid of the blanket kist and got a clout round the lug from Elsie. There were paper hats to wear and chocolates to eat, decorated with crystallised violets. Stockings hung from the mantelshelf on Christmas morning with apples, oranges and "sugar piggies" for the little ones. Jessie ate the nose and ears and other delicate parts of her pink sugar pig, while Johnie delighted in devouring the rear end. Days later, he was seen using his new penknife to pare off the floor-soiled debris from the remains of his pig's torso, prior to having another sook at it.

Mary looked healthier than ever before and Elsie was as wiry, strong and swack as ever. A sense of well-being and festive goodwill pervaded the household, spoilt only by her father wittering on about the prospect of war. He constantly talked about the strategic importance of Lerwick should conflict break out:

"The harbour's full o' German vessels, Jean, and here we're at the crossroads o' the North Sea and the Atlantic Ocean, a first class base for naval operations. These waters will be a busy thoroughfare, Jean, and it'll be a war at sea for 'is country . . . mark my words. Shetland's in a key position."

CHAPTER
7
Metamorphosis

In retrospect, the spring of 1914 brought clear signs that conflict between nations was imminent. A wireless station was being built at Sound, near the Loch of Trebister. Harbour activity was intense, with thirty-three German drifters noted in a single week and the German fishery cruiser "Poseidon" having a prominent profile. John Watt was convinced of the forthcoming war but Jean still thought him to be over-imaginative.

"The Poseidon is only studying the effects of trawling in the North Sea, Dad, so keep yer hair on."

Johnie was ten years old and already helping his father by selling fish direct to the public from the Bressay slip. On school days, he started at 7a.m. for two hours before classes, and he worked longer during his holidays. He sorted the fresh fish into 3d and 6d bundles. The "peerie Watt boy" had developed quite a reputation for giving good value: he put twelve large haddocks in a generous bundle for 1/-. In the beginning, Jean used to supervise him but he needed no overseer now. Sometimes he came home with a few coins, more often than not he had spent a bawbee on a poke of brown sugar which was tucked away in his pocket, and frequently he brought an assortment of traded foodstuffs like cabbage, tatties, and mutton.

"Foo muckle fish div ye gie them for the tatties, Johnie?" Jean quizzed him.

"Weel, Jeanie, they fill an empty 7lb corned beef tin and I exchange that for a 6d bundle. An just look whit a treat I've gotten the day . . . a coggie o' fresh milk wi' a doad o' lovely butter floatin in it."

"Aye, Jean," laughed Elsie, "I doubt they winna swick oor Johnie. He's a dab hand at dealin wi' aabody, even the toffs an' the bigwigs noo, an' he winna be fooled wi' the meally mouthed kind!"

When their income was low, Jean and Johnie spent many hours gathering whelks as far afield as Dales Voe. They sold them to R & C Robertson in exchange for a chit to purchase goods from the shop. They seldom took a cash payment because a credit note for groceries proved to be better value. It was cold hard work gathering whelks in the ebb and they were heavy to carry. Johnie, who seemed to find a simple solution to every practical problem, rigged up a pair of creels tied on to the cross-bar of an old bicycle to transport them to Lerwick.

In May, Jean signed on for her second herring season, with Nellie and Babs again. They had kept in touch by two letters from Jean's end and a thinly worded postcard from Babs. It was the spring of a new year and Jean felt vibrant, full of the joys of life. She still thought that her father was being pessimistic about a war. She had no inner inkling of a global disaster.

She felt familiar with the environment of the curing yard now and sympathised with the fresh intake of young teenage girls, nervously feeling their way around with painful fingers. She had matured greatly in the past year and was much more aware of her woman's body. She thought she had an adult's mind as well. She took pride in her appearance on the yard, always wearing a clean bibbed apron over her working clothes and tying back her hair in a coloured scarf, tucked in like a turban. She cut the legs off old stockings and pulled the tubular part over her forearms as protection against the flying sparks of salt pickle that had irritated her delicate skin the previous year. For Sundays and special occasions, she bought herself a costume, with a well cut skirt ending just above the ankle, showing off her knitted black stockings, a striped winceyette petticoat and a hat trimmed with cherries to wear to the service. She handed down her liberty bodice to her sister, Jessie, and bought lightweight lacing stays as an alternative. She felt very grown up.

She was not beautiful: from examination in the mirror, she noted that her face was asymmetrical, with one eyebrow slightly higher than the other, giving her a surprised and quizzical look. Her mouth too was a little squint but it curved easily into a friendly smile. She had a high bridge to her nose and a secret wish that it would not grow any bigger because her father had a big nose and she dreaded one like it. She had a trim, well proportioned figure and her eyes were her best attribute: hazel and long lashed with a mischievous twinkle.

She had long since learned how to use them to charm her father into her way of thinking and soon found that she had a persuasive nature with other gentlemen. Strong, direct eye contact and a few well chosen words usually did the trick. She became a favourite on the yard that year, always willing to have time for her fellow man, frequently smiling and displaying her friendly personality. Everybody liked her and she attracted frivolity and fun.

James West made two decisions that summer: the time had come for him to skipper his own vessel; and he must look for a wife, this being an economic necessity for a budding skipper, to help with line baiting, keep house, and mend and redd out the nets. He knew only too well that "no man could be a fisher, and lack a wife", but it would be wise to choose carefully. He had experienced a lifetime of nagging from his pernickety mother and the words of his father were entrenched in his mind:

> *"James, James, for sic a life,*
> *withoot a wife,*
> *and...misery when you get her!"*

He had known Jean most of her life but, recently, had become increasingly attracted to her. She seemed quite different at her work and had the most captivating eyes he'd ever seen, especially in one so young and innocent. He watched her aloofly, merely ackowledging her presence with a wave or a nod when he dressed her hands or had to deliver herring to the yard. Occasionally he let a smile flash, but quickly reined it back if anyone was looking, replacing it with a dismissive nod. He was a man of few words, like her father.

He was fully thirteen years her senior, yet still in no hurry. He could wait a while and watch the complete metamorphosis from girl to woman. However, she sensed his basic intention, although hardly a word was ever exchanged between them. She thought him a handsome and interesting man, intelligent, always reading or writing, but she was not ready to make any commitment yet. Life was sparkling with opportunities.

The young loons aboard the Shetland boats (mostly from Burra and Whalsay) were frequent visitors to the yard, unloading catches, eyeing up the girls and generally showing off. Two lads in particular, Peter Manson and his cousin, Billy Leask, were renowned for their high spirited pranks. Peter was the older of the two at twenty-one, although he did not act his age, while Billy was only sixteen, spending a summer aboard his uncle's boat for the first time. They were always capering with buckets of water, soaking each other to the skin while swilling down the deck or the fishboxes. They walked on the rows of kits rather than on the road; they rattled the bogies up the rails at a foolhardy speed and had the coopers after them at regular intervals. The resulting chase was part of the fun. The boys were wild.

The Wisemans and Jean were competing fiercely with another team for the honour of being top crew. Nellie cracked the whip even more than before: she was determined to be the fastest packer on the station. Like the best of her trade, she could comfortably handle three barrels an hour, each one holding up to a thousand herring. She shouted frequently for more fish. At times, it was difficult to keep the old lady furnished, and well nigh impossible to lose precious minutes by answering the call of nature.

Jean was rightly proud of the fact that she was now as fast as Babs and could gut and grade sixty to seventy herrings a minute, sorting them into their various size categories: smas; matties; matt fulls; fulls; and large fulls, depositing them in the appropriate tubs behind her, ready to pack. Sometimes Nellie was physically sick after hours of being bent double with her stomach constricted by the rim of the barrel. She would retire to a quiet spot on the seafront and could be heard retching loudly. Then back she always came and stooped to her task again. She had a great resilience to personal discomfort and was as tough as the skin of a dogfish.

The Wiseman crew were the victims of many a prank at the hands of the two boys, who took delight in slowing them down a little, making Nellie livid with rage. Billy Leask would take a handful of guts from one of the cougs and sprinkle them among the neatly packed herring in the barrel when her back was turned. She lost time picking the fish clean again before another layer could be added:

"Keep 'at coorse loon oot o' my barrel! Run, Jean, gie him yer boot in his backside!"

The girls pretended to chastise the boys but could not help laughing aloud and joining in their high spirits. The sheer exuberance of youth unleashed bubbled from all four of them.

The tormenting and leg pulling and the mock rage became a game and Jean looked forward to the boys coming ashore. They'd creep up on Babs and Jean as they bent over their farlins and slap a herring on the back of their necks so that they shrieked with the shock of the cold wet fish on their warm exposed skin. When things were quiet, they chatted to the boys, or about them, in the rest-room or on the Gremista hill behind the station, where they often took their knitting. Jean was an expert at reproducing the "rope", the "barleycorn" and the "links of love," typical patterns of the scotch ganseys, but she could also turn her hand to Fair Isle. She picked up the new designs from Peter or Billy's sweaters. She enjoyed the closeness of counting the stitches from the body of the wearer while having an excuse for being tactile. They got to know the boys very well.

Occasionally they were lucky enough to have a Saturday afternoon off and sometimes met the boys in the town. There was no privacy, only the chaotic scramble of Lerwick's humanity: shoppers darting in and out the doors of Laing, Porteous and Stout, Chemists; Stove and Smith, Ironmongers; R & C Robertson, Grocers, the numerous clothes shops, Leisk & Sandison, Sinclair Johnson, Smith and Robertson. There were street vendors flaunting dubious wares of all descriptions, useless lotions and potions jostling for space with authentic goods; musicians busking at the Market Cross; inebriated tramps and characters like cockroaches; children playing marbles in corners of the road; town toffs and beggars.

Beside Fort Charlotte, the mysterious Arab manned his stall, open suitcases spread around his feet, coloured carpets displayed against the high wall. The beauty of his wares was in stark contrast to his lean, mean look. His name was "Hadi Adi al Khatib" but the local kids called him "Haddie and Chips". He didn't like children much. They congregated around his chattering monkey and he lost no time in disciplining them, especially if parental supervision was absent. Jean stopped to admire a particular oriental rug: it was hand knotted and the richly coloured designs were enchanting, like a magic carpet. How she would love to own such a beautiful thing . . . though the price was way beyond her reach. It would take months of gutting fish to pay for such a luxury.

She always found the range of Lerwick's smells overpowering: butcher's raw meat, baker's hot yeasty bread, cabbage water stench, stale beer and rancid sweat. At the foot of some of the lanes, there was the strong musky odour of male urine and she often had to step over a vile trickle of liquid, unknown putrid fluids that oozed out of the mouth of the close. There was polish and quality, dereliction and decay, all mixed together in a heady cocktail of living town.

One particular Saturday, the girls had been window shopping and were skipping along behind the Salvation Army procession, keeping step to the tambourines, when a mangy dog darted in front of them, nearly tripping up Babs. It was intent on chasing an equally mangy bitch and lost no time in mounting her in full view of the crowded street. An incensed shopkeeper ran out with a bucket of dirty water slops and poured it over the coupling pair, causing the bitch to yelp loudly as the mongrel tried to disengage himself.

The girls giggled and hurried out of earshot of the embarrassment, followed by Peter and Billy, who had chanced upon them just minutes before. Nobody mentioned the dogs but all were quietly impressed by the awesome power of basic animal instinct. The foursome walked past a drunk and disorderly man who was well dressed. Some problem had likely led him to drink and the drink had given him other problems: he had unsightly food remnants ingrained in his teeth and a stained tie. He slouched beside a pile of vomit and shouted to Jean with pungent boosy breath:

"Hi, darling! How about a kiss then?" .

They laughed, judging him to be at least a half bottle off the straight and narrow. They hurried towards the clear clean sound of a steam whistle blowing in the harbour. Gideon Pouffe stood at the Cross, filled with the other kind of spirit. A few stopped to listen, some mocked, children accepted pandrops and hastily retreated. Scrunched up texts littered the flagstones. Gulls squabbled over a pile of fishheads and small boys dangled lines in the water.

As they passed the Tolbooth, James West doffed his cap to them and Jean smiled briefly, before turning her attention back to her companions. I fear I've waited too long, James thought, watching the youngsters, hearing their laughter...I should've approached her quicker. He sighed.

Before the day was done, in the early evening, the foursome had a group photograph taken at Ramsay's and Peter asked Babs to walk out with him a week on Sunday. Billy was more shy about things, so it was Babs who suggested that they could all go on an outing together, after the service. Perhaps they could take a picnic?

47

8

Holm, Sweet Holm

The girls spent every spare half hour from Thursday till Saturday preparing for the picnic. The whitewashed brick fireplace in their hut was stocked up well with coal, and oatcakes, pancakes and scones were baked on a griddle. A meat and potato pie was made in a pastry case as a change from their staple diet of fish. Hard boiled eggs, a slice of cheese, and home-made lemonade completed the feast. They were out to impress with their culinary skills.

Sunday dawned cool, grey and drizzly and disappointment set in at the prospect of the picnic being postponed. However, after the morning service the sun blinked, the drookled rooftops and puddles steamed visibly and a perfect rainbow appeared. The outlook brightened as Jean had seen it do on so many similar schizophrenic Shetland days. The sky cleared to the south west. There was only a mild breeze.

Peter knocked at two minutes past noon. Jean was amazed at the transformation. She had never seen the boys in their Sunday best before, faces polished up like shiny red apples. The mutual admiration caused an awkward silence on the doorstep, broken by Jean bursting into a fit of giggles. This defused the situation, and everybody laughed.

"Where do you fancy goin then, lasses?" said Peter, falling into a chivalrous mode appropriate to his clothes and taking the basket of goodies from Babs.

"Weel, we've seen plenty of Gremista these past weeks, and the Green Head is aye crawling wi' dozes o' folk, so hoo aboot takin us tae see the sooth end o' the toon?" Babs said.

"Oh aye, Peter," said Jean, "I like the Sands o' Soond and it'll be a fine walk the day."

No objections were raised and the foursome set off at a leisurely pace, Babs and Peter walking several yards ahead to maintain an element of privacy. They walked slowly past the herring yards, picking their way between the numerous salt puddles, peppered with scales and patterned with rainbows of oil. They were as happy as the buzzing bluebottles that scavenged around the debris, crawling over the barrels and the green slimy wooden railings that edged the steps leading up to the huts. Their route took them up Fleet Street, on to the track skirting the Clickimin Loch and the Picts' Broch, passing Hayfield House across the water and then over the stiles into the open fields of Sound.

It was the end of June and there were a few families with children at the beach. Laughter echoed over the sand dunes and there was a gleeful splashing of little bare feet in the shallows. They found a lovely spot at the mouth of a peaty burn some distance south of the sands. A few thatched cottages stood nearby, so picturesque compared to town dwellings. They ate heartily and laughed at everything and nothing at all. Afterwards, Babs and Peter wandered off around the bay, towards the Grotty Buckie.

Billy and Jean lingered by the burn.

"I bet du's never tickled a troot, Jean," he said, not giving her time to answer. " A'm brocht oot mony a shinin beauty fae under da broo o' da Weisdale burn."

"Geng on then, let's see ye get een?"

"Och, du kens dis trickle o' water is far ower peerie tae support troots."

"Excuses, excuses!" she teased, walking off to pick wild orchids in shades of purple, pink and lilac that grew in abundance in the marshy field nearby. She felt very much at home with the boy, as if she had known him all her life. They made daisy chains and Billy picked the petals off a dandelion one by one, saying "She loves me, she loves me not..." and cheating by pulling off two together when the game of chance was not in his favour. He told her that dandelions would make her "pee the bed" so only boys should handle them.

Later in the afternoon the teenagers were drawn back towards the sandy beach where a few straggling children still dabbled their sparrow legs in the water, oblivious to the impatient umpteenth call of parents that it was time to go home. Bright fronds of seaweed still clung to wet little hands with blue tinged fingers that felt no cold. There were letters written in the sand with a stick, spelling the name "Val"; the remains of a grandiose sandcastle representing hours of parental peace and quiet; a wet sock discarded and a treasure trove of shells and stones, piled in a heap, lost but not forgotten. A smell of fresh waar filled the air.

"Look, Billy, the tide's gone oot. 'At wee island's become a peninsula!"

"It's called a holm, Jean, but yun wan is no a real holm, I

49

suppose, if we can walk oot tae it at low tide. Dir's a lok o' real holms in Whiteness whaar I cum fae. I'll tak dee tae see dem wan day, if du liks?"

They crossed the damp sandy spit, past a little pool left behind by the retreating tide. The water was calm and translucent, revealing an underwater world of darting silver bellies and scurrying hermit crabs, breathtakingly beautiful in its purity and simplicity. They clambered up the rocks to the flat grassy top. Fledgeling terns and gulls scurried from their intruding feet in the long grass, or froze to a living stone, camouflaged against the rocks. The plateau was moving with young life, living proof of the perpetual need for species to reproduce their own kind. Billy picked up a stone and threw it at a marauding great skua:

"Git oot o' dat, du heathen bonxie!" he shouted. "I hae nae time fur yun birds," he said. "Dey pick aff the young dunters one by one, and cause havoc wi' da newborn lambs."

The bird fled. The teenagers held hands and lay on their stomachs in the long grass.

Billy was easy to relate to. He told her of his childhood, his home in Whiteness, his family, his interest in motors and all kinds of engineering. He explained that he was only aboard with his cousin Peter and uncle Ertie for one summer, and that was enough:

"I wis as seeck as a dug. I doot, lass, A'm mair at home wi' da land as da sea," he confided.

"If I'd been a man, I believe I'd a geen tae sea," she said.

"Weel, no me, Jean. A'm gain tae da mainland shune, tae serve me time as a mechanic in wan o' da big Aberdeen garages. Me faider is fixed it up wi' een o' his cronies dere . . . Some day, I hop tae hae a business o' me ain."

"So, when d'ye go awa?" she asked, in a matter-of-fact voice, pretending that it was of marginal interest to her.

"A'm no really dat sure, but shunner rather dan later . . . I've had twartree fierce clashes wi' me midder aboot it. Shö wants me tae study medicine lik me faider, no messy engines."

His Shetland accent was broader than Peter's, a result of his rural upbringing, and yet he had an easy flowing way of explaining things when he tried seriously. Jean had never talked so much in all her life. Conversation had been minimal at home, there seemed little need for it. It was wonderful to communicate so freely.

She could see a deeper level to the frivolous, devil-may-care, weekday Billy. She liked this private image very much. He was her first sweetheart, she thought, her heart giving a little flutter of excitement as she looked at him through the waving heads of the yellow green grasses. Billy was chewing a straw. He was so boyishly handsome with his dark thick hair and deep brown eyes, pools of secrecy, inviting. She wondered if she could see his soul if she concentrated hard and stared into those eyes and she was afraid that she would. He had a fine stubble of youthful whiskers partly covering the dimple on his chin and such long eyelashes for a boy, like spiders. He had a golden tan and a clear complexion. She wondered if the tiny blemish (that seemed enormous) on her forehead was visible or still covered by her hair as she had arranged it earlier. She allowed herself to admire his lean strong body, glimpsing a warm smooth bit of chest at the neck of his shirt and wondering what it would be like to put her cheek against it.

Conscious of her scrutiny, he picked up a handful of the sandy earth.

"How does du feel aboot Shetland soil, Jean. Is it home tae dee noo?"

"Aye, Billy, Shetland is hame. Hame, sweet hame, . . . or should I say holm, sweet holm?" she giggled.

"I'm gled, Jean. I hiv a deep sense o' belongin' here, and it's very strong right dis meenit. It's a queer thought, but, in a wye, I wish we could die, right here and noo. Things'll maybe niver be dis perfect again."

Jean met his eyes, understood this strange morbid contradiction, and squeezed his hand. He kissed her then, and his mouth was sweet and warm and slightly open. She thought she was going to die. They were acutely aware of each other's bodies, but their interest was inquisitive: their yearning for closer physical contact was infinitely more innocent than the ripe lust that Jean had witnessed in the hut last summer. Yet the anticipation of unknown pleasures to come was thrilling.

I wonder if sins of the mind are as bad as actual sins? she thought. Then she said, "I hear Peter calling."

Peter was in a joyous mood and Babs looked pink and radiant. All agreed that the day had been a great success as they set off towards Lerwick.

"Peter is going to mak us a cuppie o' tea in his hoose at the Hillheed on the wye hame, Jean," said Babs proudly, holding on to his arm.

51

It was a grand house, belonging to his mother's family who were well-to-do merchants (and who had not been too pleased with her choice of a Burra fisherman as a husband). Peter showed them into the front room. On the floor, Jean saw the beautiful oriental rug from Haddie and Chips's stall. Peter seemed surprised to find his mother entertaining his auntie Agnes. A pleasant looking middle-aged gentleman sat in an armchair in the corner, looking slightly bored. He was clearly Billy's father, bearing the unmistakable Leask hallmark, a dimple on his chin.

"Oh, sorry Mam, I thought you were oot," Peter stammered, "This is Babs Wiseman and Jean Watt . . . we've been on a picnic." Turning to the girls, he said " My mother, Margaret . . . and Billy's mother, Agnes . . . and his father, William, Dr. Leask."

The two women looked similar, each with her hair pulled back into a tight bun, sharpening already stern features. They had dark little eyes, with sparse lashes. They were both dressed immaculately and ultra composed. The one called Agnes glowered at Jean, examining her appearance methodically, with a caustic eye like old Nellie checking the top tier of her barrel for rejects. A grudging greeting was nodded in their general direction. The man stood up in preparation to shake hands but his intention was overruled by Margaret's sharp voice:

"Weel Peter, Agnes and Willie have been here for da afternoon. Dey wir hopin tae see peerie Billy afore gyain back tae Whiteness. It wis inconsiderate o' you no to say whaar you wir going. You've been awa the whole day!"

Jean was suddenly aware that she was staring rudely at Dr. Leask. He was familiar. She had a distinct feeling of *deja vu* and it nagged like an invisible kipper bone. He met her gaze . . . and she knew! He had the same soul-piercing eyes as the alien man in her strange dream. She felt a coldness in the soles of her feet and it crept up her legs like freezing pickle, settling in the base of her spine.

"Come on, lasses, we'll go into the kitchen and make some tea, and leave Billy to spaek to his fok." Peter ushered them out of the frost-bitten room.

Jean felt out of place and unwelcome in this posh house. She had always sensed atmosphere and knew instictively when people were warm and when they were cold. She hardly touched her tea. The door stayed ajar, allowing Agnes's raised voice to be heard clearly:

"But whit kind o' lasses is yun, Billy? Dir Scottie fishwives, dat's whit dey ir! You dinna want tae be associated wi' da liks o' yun! Dey'll drag you doon! I'm gled du'll no be hingin aroond Lerook muckle langer, boy!"

Peter jumped up, red faced with embarrassment, and shut the door. Jean rose to her feet, too, with all the adult dignity she could muster. She informed Babs that they were leaving now. She felt the tears of the rejected child prick at her eyelids, the hot retaliation of her pride fighting them back. She minded the warning in her dream, and her grandmother's words echoed in her head. Her self-confidence, which had soared like a laverick during the day, was squashed. She had to get out.

As she hurried along the Hillhead, desperately trying to escape the anguish, tears boiling on her cheeks, she ran straight into James West.

"Good . . . fit's adee wi' ye, Jean?"

"I'm fine, Mr West," she choked, ". . . but I maun get hame." She ran on and he stared after her.

In her despair, he sensed hope after all.

It was a few weeks later, on Saturday, 2nd August, that the Territorial Army was called out. Britain declared war on Germany on 4th August and all German vessels left Lerwick harbour in a great hurry.

The herring season was in full swing, but it came to an abrupt and premature halt. The curers were left with 36,000 barrels on their yards. Having lost the lucrative German market, there were frantic efforts to find trade routes into Russia via Archangel. Jean, Babs and Nellie were left with a low season's earnings.

Following the fateful day of the picnic, Jean saw nothing more of Billy. She was relieved. However, shortly after the outbreak of hostilities, she received an unexpected letter with an Aberdeen postmark:

"Dear Jean,
I am sorry that our day out ended so abruptly. I want to let you know that I have left Shetland to start my three year apprenticeship. I thought it was best to get away from my mother for a while, since we do not see eye to eye on many things. In fact, we had another bad row before I left and I have vowed never to return, but time will tell. I am stubborn, Jean, so it may be a while before I come back. As you will recall, I am very interested in modern motor vehicles

53

as well as diesel engines for boats and who knows? I may get engineering experience in the war if there is still some action when I have served my time. I do not think it will last long though.

I know I am very young and my mother thinks that I do not know my own mind but, like my father, I have always made my mind up quickly and seldom reverse my decisions. Jean, I will come back home when I have finished my training and my family dispute has faded. I am very fond of you and will marry you one day if you will wait for me. I am not much of a one for writing. My father says that true friendships survive time and trials of all sorts and do not need the written word to prop them up. Shallow, trivial or false relationships will fall by the wayside, despite a constant stream of letters.

With this belief in mind, I will close now,
Yours respectfully,

Billy Leask
P.S. Please eat this letter because it is soppy and I do not want sued for breach of promise!"

Jean crumpled the page, then smoothed it out and read it again. She knew this was the end of their relationship. She resolved to resign herself to a cautious coexistence with these damned islanders. Never again would she seek a Shetland suitor! She would stick to her own kind. Yet her tender heart still ached with the poignant memory of the carefree summer . . . and the day on the holm, sweet holm.

The years of the war were bleak for the fishermen as they were for the rest of the community. Many enlisted. The government lost no time in sending mobilisation papers to reservists. John Watt and James West, who already served in the Royal Naval Reserve, were called to duty. Many brave young men were never to see their homes again.

Several fishing vessels were taken over by the Admiralty for minesweeping and other general purposes and half of the country's fishermen were put in uniform. The Germans laid mines in the approach channels to Lerwick harbour so that the minesweepers had to go out each morning to clear a two by twelve mile shipping channel.

Three months after the outbreak of war, Lerwick was established as an examination base for auxiliary patrol vessels. This meant that all boats going to and from Faroe, Iceland and the White Sea had to rendezvous for instructions. There were 250 calling vessels during the single month of December.

Over the next few years, the harbour rippled with tension: a steady stream of battle-scarred warships arrived; crippled trading ships limped in for refuge; and wounded men of many nationalities stretched Lerwick's medical resources to the limit.

Alexandra Wharf and the Fishmarket were taken over for military activities. The remaining fishing activity was severely restricted and also became extremely dangerous. In June 1915, German submarines sank 16 drifters off the Skerries, leaving 140 survivors to be picked up, by the two vessels that they inadvertently left intact.

———

The enterprising Johnie established a small fish round during these years, buying the odd box of fish directly from the boats, smoking them himself, and delivering fresh filleted and smoked products to areas in the town. His clientele varied from the toffs to odd bods of all nationalities and some whose origins could not be determined by accent. He was not a talkative boy and did not associate much with his customers. However, he supplied good quality fish and established regulars.

One of his strangest patrons was Bella Beastie from Pig Street. She was a witchy kind of a creature who hardly ever came out, leaving instead a plate with sixpence on her doorstep. Johnie filled the dish, took the coin and knocked loudly on the door, lest a scavenging cat should pinch her dinner. She was certainly a weird lady, a tall, thin, haunting woman. Folk said she was the herald of doom and to "beware of her showing herself tae ye in broad daylight, for sic a sightin was fair sure to mean a death or a drownin."

The first time Johnie passed Bella Beastie's open window, he was startled by a loud voice saying: "Ye buggerahell.Ye buggerahell.Ye buggerahell." It was a green and red parrot that swore worse than any drunk! The bairns in Pig Street fair tormented that parrot, prigging with it to learn new swear words. The witchy wife intrigued Johnie. He imagined her as having strange dark powers and he was a little feart of her. It was rare that he got a good look at her, yet she was never unkind to him, often handing him out a piece of bread and jam with a delicate disembodied hand from the sanctuary of her dimly lit home.

Johnie's family trait of silent communication was

55

compounded by the shyness of adolescence and he became a bit of a loner, a sort of small business recluse. Jean, on the other hand, continued to develop an outgoing personality. She had always been close to her brother but now they grew apart.

Billy Leask was a million miles away. For many people, the world had fallen apart.

CHAPTER

9

Canary Condition

When the need came for women war workers, Jean saw her chance to see a bit of the world south of Shetland. In the summer of 1915, she wrote in answer to an urgent call for girls to staff the jute factories of Dundee but then quickly volunteered for munitions work once she got there. She started her munitions training course in the Spring of 1916. It lasted four weeks.

There she met women from all over Scotland and the Isles and from all walks of life: domestic servants; farmhands; dressmakers; clerical workers; schoolteachers. Many were unfit for the work and showed signs of fatigue and stiffness after the long shifts, but compared to the duration of her sessions gutting herring with the Wiseman team, Jean found the shifts only moderately tiring.

She was soon moved to a small factory on the outskirts of London where she worked from 7 a.m. till 5.30 p.m., with an hour for lunch and the chance of overtime in the evenings. It was cold in the premises and many of the women huddled together near the coke buckets that were placed strategically around the open space of the factory floor. The heat source was very localised and the fumes were unpleasant, but Jean adjusted to the chilly work. It was not as bad as the open yards at Yarmouth in November and at least there was a roof over her head. She was paid fourpence halfpenny an hour for a fifty-four hour week.

She did not like London with its massive queues for food and coal, with its big water rats from the Thames that infested the underground tube stations.

She was relieved to be transferred to the National Cordite factory in Gretna. She was there for six months, along with eleven thousand other women. It was on her very first day there that she met Jennifer Brown. Jean had hardly time to unpack her suitcase in the dormitory when the matron burst in, waving a pair of artificial silk stockings and shouting:

"Where's Jennifer Brown? . . . if I've warned her once, I've

57

given her a thousand warnings . . . she'll have all privileges restricted for a week this time!"

"Oh, God . . . the old battleaxe means it . . . I'm for it now," muttered the pretty redhead beside the next bed. The matron advanced, brandishing the stockings.

"Well, Madam . . . are these yours? . . . You know perfectly well that semi-transparent stockings are not allowed in this establishment."

"They're mine," said Jean impulsively, "I didn't know that they were against the rules. I'm sorry."

The masculine looking matron stared at her and then said: "Humph . . . You're the new girl . . . well put these unsuitable things away and don't let me find them in the laundry room again.

Jennifer . . . find this lass a copy of the rule book." She turned on her heel and stomped out.

From that incident sprung a friendship that grew closer as they read and ridiculed the rule book. On the matter of clothing, garters were not advised and woollen stockings only were allowed. Girls were asked to stitch elastic to the bottom of their corsets, a button to the elastic strip and a band of ribbon to the top of knitted or cashmere stockings, which were thus "suspended". Jennifer had great fun modelling the finished product to the other girls in the dormitory.

Knickers were to be tweed or cloth and with closed legs and a removable lining for washing each week. Girls were advised to bathe more frequently at certain periods of the month and to use a mackintosh patch "to prevent accidents". Jean opted for the modern idea of calico band loops sewn front and back and disposable sanitary towels.

Jennifer came from a small village outside Glasgow and was a year older than Jean. She was a little on the plump side, with red rosy cheeks and a smatter of attractive freckles over the bridge of her button nose. Her hair was naturally curly and she had an exuberance that was hard for a young man to resist. She was a jolly, uninhibited, rough-edged girl, with a great sense of humour and strong sympathies for the suffrage movement.

They continued to share the same dormitory in one of the specially built government hostels in Carlisle. The bottom floor was reserved for male workers and the upper floor housed women. However, there was always some mixing of the sexes at the weekly socials on Wednesday evenings and at the government-run pub, where it was acceptable for girls to go for the occasional celebration and where snack food was served to all patrons. The hostel matron kept a watchful eye on the flock of young females, now far removed from their often sheltered family backgrounds and consequently not subject to the usual religious and social restraints.

Despite this firm pastoral approach, and the lack of young men after the universal military conscription in May 1916, evidence of illegitimate "war babies" appeared from time to time and unhappy pregnant girls left. A few got married to their sweethearts, although many of these men were called again to the front, never to return.

The months at the Gretna factory were a great revelation to Jean on the subjects of welfare and morality. During her first week at the hostel, she was given a pamphlet to read, written by the Welfare Superintendent, Lilian A. Evans. It covered many sensible areas, from advice on how often to take baths to how to eradicate lice. Jennifer read aloud to Jean the section on the subject of "personal diseases", stopping to laugh at frequent intervals and especially at the ending . . . "it is not fitting to provide details. Any woman with unusual soreness or discharge should seek medical help without delay."

She also encouraged Jean's awareness of many current problems. On one occasion she took her to a suffragette meeting where a Miss Maud Royden spoke on the issue of female morality and the growing problem of the "war babies". Jean was fascinated by the eloquence of the woman's lecture and longed to be able to express her own opinions with such common sense and fluency. Some of the words stayed with her for a long time afterwards:

"It is the grey and sordid monotony of the badly paid girl, engaged in some unskilled, uninteresting and monotonous work, just at that age when romance and adventure make her demand from life colour and interest and beauty and love. This is often the real cause of the mischief."

Jean longed for colour and beauty and love in a relationship with a man....with her Billy - but he was gone and she would never see him again. She was almost sure that James West was wooing her in his quiet way but there remained an element of doubt. He looked at her differently when he had come to see her before she left Shetland. He had been on a fortnight's leave and was going straight back to the

Navy. She wasn't sure what to make of him. He was a fascinating man, learned, older . . . but so silent. Unlike Jennifer, who had several suitors in tow at any one time, Jean was not interested in any of the young men whom she met in Gretna, although some were pleasant enough.

The common leisure facilities were very good at the hostel and she had a wonderful opportunity to use the free library and she learnt to play chess. There were many board games and a sewing machine, even a gramophone. She spent much of her time writing home and reading avidly. She particularly enjoyed works by the Manchester journalist Harold Brighouse, especially his play "Hindle Wakes" about a factory girl who refused to marry the boss's son after becoming pregnant. Jean admired the strength of character of the heroine and tried to adopt a few of her finer principles. Another influential book was Eleanor Glynn's "Three Weeks", branded by many as sordid and immoral, but thought-provoking in suggesting that the female sexual appetite may be as great if not greater than the male.

Jean wondered if indeed such an idea could be true. She was curious yet remarkably innocent about sexual matters. She was intrigued by her own body yet terrified to explore it. She was put off effectively by a handbook, given to her by Jennifer as a source of amusement and written by Agnes Baden-Powell, originally designed for girl guides, on the forbidden subject of female masturbation:

"All secret bad habits are evil and dangerous, lead to hysteria and lunatic asylums and serious illness is the result. Evil practices dare not face an honest person; they lead you to blindness, paralysis and loss of memory."

She read many practical and helpful books like "Housekeeping on Twenty Five Shillings a Week for a Family of Five." She wondered if ever she would have a family of her own and purchased a copy of the book for a penny and put it in her bottom drawer for future reference.

The girls were given a free pint of milk each day when on TNT duty in order to keep them fit and in the vain hope of counteracting the side effects of the tri-nitrotoluene, jokingly referred to as the "canary condition". Those affected turned a sickly shade of jaundice yellow and coughed a bitter tasting yellow phlegm. Some had nausea and headaches and others developed a rash. After a short spell of this work, the canary girls were quite easy to recognise and were treated with respect and concern by members of the general public. It was not unusual for a seat on a crowded bus to be made available for a canary, or for the girls to receive preferential treatment when queuing.

The factory work was monotonous and great care had to be exercised when handling the yellow chemical. Being a natural gossip, Jennifer could not adjust to working with her mouth shut, although all workers were advised to keep silent except at break times because the fine powder got into the mouth and rotted the teeth. To minimise the yellowing of their skin, a form of barrier cream, known simply as "Hypo", was distributed.

The silent atmosphere increased the monotony of the tasks themselves. There was also a small but finite risk of explosion from any form of sparks. Consequently, smoking was strictly taboo and there were special wooden walkways between the various buildings to eliminate grit coming in on the feet, which were clad in overshoes at all times. Spark-proof implements were used to handle the powder itself, including leather buckets and a brass scoop. It was most unlike the noisy, singing, banging atmosphere of a good going herring yard and Jean especially missed the working banter.

It was November 1916 when she got affected by "canary condition" and was sent home on sick leave. She never returned. Although she kept in touch with Jennifer for a while, her friend was not the writing type. Jean did not worry about this because she was quite sure that they had the kind of close comradship that could withstand time and distance. Jean later heard that Jennifer had been badly injured in a nitro-glycerine explosion in the same factory early in 1917.

It was the Spring before Jean really resumed normal health. James West called to see her again during his short home leave but she remained uncertain about his intentions, although she enjoyed walking out with him and felt quite proud of their association.

There was plenty of work to keep her occupied with the war effort at home. She helped with small scale fish curing when she could, assisted with laundry for the servicemen based locally, and accompanied Elsie on her trips to collect sphagnum moss. The moss was collected from the sides of burns on the outskirts of Lerwick and the countryside. It was used to dress wounds and almost 2,000 bags each year were shipped from Shetland. As she collected the soft, damp, delicate greenery, she wondered whose wound might benefit from it . . . Would it end up on a Shetland soldier? She hoped that James would not be wounded. She wondered where Billy Leask was now.

The increase in harbour activity was colossal. Jean remembered her father telling her that Shetland would be a major thoroughfare for ships and he was proved right. Around 200 ships per month represented the flow rate before the war but now that figure had increased to over 1000 per month passing through Bressay Sound, more activity than any other port in Britain.

10

Mud, Blood and Michelle

Billy Leask returned home only once during his three year apprenticeship. The trip was a disaster. His mother nagged non-stop, especially when she heard that he'd called on Jean Watt. To make matters worse, Jean's mother informed him that Jean was working in a factory in Carlisle, and the grandmother made a point of telling him that Jean was courting a fellow called James West. Elsie firmly believed that Jean should stick to her own kind.

Billy wrote a few times to his father after that but the rift between him and Agnes was slow to heal. Thus, when his training was finished, along with a friend and fellow engineer called Red Geordie, he decided to join up. The Royal Engineers were desperate for trained recruits, having expanded rapidly since 1914 when there were only 78 units. By 1917, there were almost 1000 units, staffed by a quarter of a million men, a proportional increase greater than any other in the armed forces. All types of trained engineers were sought.

The range of duties performed by the Royal Engineers included water boring operations, land drainage, tunnelling works, surveying, special camouflage projects, railway works, signals, and transportation. Billy and Geordie were drafted to France to serve with a mobile field company, whose general remit was to complete new tunnelling works, erect Nissen huts at pre-arranged sites and upgrade reclaimed trenches and communication channels as the front line shifted. They were also required to provide support for the infantry divisions, by answering specific requests for assistance, so providing a technical troubleshooting service.

Billy's first impression of France was not endearing. They arrived in Le Havre docks early in the evening. It was misty and the heavy yellowish fug had an unsavoury taint. They were led through unlit sections of a shabby town, past equally shabby inhabitants, most of them looking lost and forlorn, like drained coffee cups. An old man with a stump for a left leg begged outside a public house and a dirty faced boy of about eight years old pimped for his older sister in the entrance of a narrow street, his pidgin English giving a fairly basic description of her talents.

The Harfleur base camp was more welcoming, being organised and informative. They were not there long, only long enough to unwind from the journey before their company was transported inland. Red Geordie had acquired a copy of "The Mudlark", a service newspaper printed by the 23rd Division. It was not full of the horror of war but attempted to suggest an artistic and humorous side. During the journey, Geordie laughed at the limericks and jokes, occasionally reading them aloud:

"Look at this one, Bill . . . It's called Striking Impressions. 'And what struck you about the Ypres battle?' asked the dear old lady. 'Shrapnel, lady!' Ha, ha, ha . . ."

Their journey took them closer and closer to the flashing and rumble of the relentless guns. It was like travelling into the centre of a rotten land, the cottages by the roadside getting more and more dilapidated as they proceeded to the heart of the sore, the flare lights and hollow whizbangs coming ever nearer. The map reference took them to a place near Armentières, close to the front line.

Each man carried an identification disc and his own equipment. The 60lbs pack included a motley assortment of supplies: basic items for personal hygiene, a greatcoat, a waterproof sheet, a set of hand tools including an entrenching implement, a trench periscope, a tin of grease, a rifle and 150 rounds of ammunition, a less than effective first-aid dressing, and a useless respirator. In addition to these items, and following the advice of a friend in Aberdeen who had been to the front, Billy and Geordie shared a few extras, including a "Tommies cooker" (a tin of solid paraffin with a cooking ring), a bottle of whale oil for rubbing their feet, an emergency supply of toffee and a tin of cocoa.

Normal practice in their unit was to serve six days on a particular trench duty, prior to a day or two of leave before a transfer to another task. Good mechanical engineers were in short supply and Billy and Red were frequently sent to other units to fix faulty machine guns, generators and other military accessories. It was not unusual for them to be missing from their mother squadron for up to a week at a time.

The reasons for leaving home seemed trivial now in the cold light of the trenches. Why on earth had he ever thought that the war would be good experience for a budding engineer? How did he ever imagine that the combat would be romantic and honourable?

The trenches stank worse than any byre, worse than the dungheaps and open sewers that ran through the most notorious of Lerwick's slum lanes. The smell was difficult to describe but there were strong elements of gas, nauseating and ineffective disinfectant, blood and latrine fumes, the strong stale urine of men and horses.

Although he had not yet served a whole year, Billy was already war weary and in an advanced state of depression. His feet were wet and swollen and his boots had not been off for a week. His legs were damp and chafed up to the knees and his oily hands were sticky with clay from the sides of the communication trench. He had been sent to contact trench headquarters for engineer duties of some sort but he was having some difficulty with directions. It was September 1918 though he was uncertain of the exact date and it did not seem to matter anyway. The war had gone on for an eternity. It was as if he had lived a strange double life: one that now seemed sweet and full of caring with few troubles, just silly minor squabbles of no consequence whatsoever . . . it seemed long ago, like a dream . . . and then this hell of an existence where whole sections of his body and mind went to sleep in order to cope with the everyday traumas of official carnage.

Friends were a luxury that the weak-hearted could not afford. Red Geordie had been his friend, a big strong Highlander with an earthy sense of humour, always making up songs to the popular tunes, like "Tipperary", but with rude words, just the tonic for failing spirits. Always joking about the equipment "issued by collar-and-tie idiots! Dinna ken their arse frae their elbow! Look at this gas mask . . . it widna keep oot a wet fart!" He'd been right there, and as for the instructions that accompanied the bloody things, well . . . they issued revised guidelines every few weeks on pink paper with an "urgent" heading, but the update often completely contradicted the earlier caveats. Red Geordie had carefully examined the different kinds of respirators around. There was the one with the chemically treated, gauze filled pad tied across the mouth which simply didn't keep out the German gas. Then there was the greasy grey thing like the sleeve off a greatcoat with the talc window, which was invariably cracked and leaked at the stitching anyway. Useless, was the verdict, especially after seeing the straggling survivors of a gas attack, ash-faced and choking in their helmets, with their buttons tarnished a sickening green and their lungs wheezing a painful future of uncertain duration.

Geordie had lived life to the full. He had frequented the "Blue Lamp" whore-house for officers, always trying to drag Billy along to meet the richest women in France with the fancy bed manners. Billy could never bring himself to go with a woman who serviced half a battalion in one night, yet he didn't want to die a virgin. It was Red who adapted the trench periscope for peeking around corners and it was the two of them who dissected the unexploded German canister. A fascinating device it was: a two gallon drum with an inner container full of pink, strong smelling explosive paste, a bit like marzipan, and the space between the two skins of the canister packed with every manner of metal debris, including rusty screws and nails, bits of lead piping, spent bullets, hinges, what appeared to be the guts of an old clock with cog wheels and springs, and a full set of false teeth.

It was only a week previously, while on an exercise shifting the position of a couple of strategically placed machine guns, that they had been hit by particularly heavy fire. They had heard the familiar "Whoo..ooo..ooo..CRASH!" as the shells approached and the two of them had thrown themselves flat on their stomachs...but it was too late for Red. Billy heard the groans of him before he turned him over. His chest had been opened like a can of bully beef and part of his face torn apart by flying shrapnel. He had endured great pain, but still his humour bubbled through the horror:

" . . . Reckon it was . . . them false Jerry teeth that hit me, Billy, . . . or maybe . . . the springs of that bloody cuckoo clock."

Billy had given him his private supply of five small morphia pellets, a present from his father for a dire emergency, and he had covered him with his waterproof cape to hide the blood oozing from the wound. Red had died and Billy had cried before the stretcher bearers came and shifted the body off the wooden duckboards to clear the trench, leaving behind only a bloodstained sandbag. The horrors of war were strangely diluted after that, because Billy switched great parts of himself off. He looked at, but did not see, the man who blew his own brains out with his rifle, the rat trailing a lump of human liver. He lived with, but did not get close to the men who snatched at fitful sleep, cried over letters from mothers or sweethearts, chain smoked with shaking fingers and crunched lice between their thumbnails. His closest friend became the trench cat, Traitor Tom, a fat feline with more than nine lives and with dinner dates on both sides of No-Man's Land.

He was shaken into reality by a booming English voice: "Are you the Jock Sapper who knows about truck engines?"

He looked into a channel to his left to see an officer of the 47th Division peeping out of a dug-out. He was glad to have made contact so quickly. These unfamiliar rabbit-warren trenches were difficult to navigate. He didn't know the topography of this particular area and he could have rambled around in blind alleys for long enough.

"Yes, sir. Sapper Leask reporting fur duty tae trench battalion headquarters, . . . sir". Billy gave a half-hearted salute, uncertain what rank of officer he was addressing but not wishing to take any chances.

"Come in, Leask. Time for a cup of tea and a tot of rum. Then I'll take you to the problem. It's one of our heavy lorries. Carrying vital supplies, you know, and it's broken down in a damned awkward spot. Holding the entire bloody show up! Jolly good to hear one of you chaps was nearby. Not many of us familiar with these new-fangled machines, what! Prefer horses m'self!" He patted Billy on the back and led him down.

He could hardly credit the level of comfort. It had papered walls and easy chairs . . . there was even a gramophone and a whisky decanter, and a squint home-made sign on the wall read "Home, Sweet Home". Billy experienced a brief spasm of "holmsickness". He banished this nostalgic feeling by concentrating on the rest of his plush surroundings. It was hard to reconcile this sanctuary with the basic hovels of his own battalion. Here, one could imagine civilian life again, were it not for the relentless noise and vibration of the guns. These were constant reminders that the nightmare was real. Yet humour was there despite everything. He read a notice nailed to a board. It had been taken from the "Aussie" magazine:

"AUSTRALIAN BEER FOR SALE

The Australian Beer Co. is pleased to announce to members
of the AIF serving in France that
Best Brands of Australian Beer
may be obtained from

hotels in NSW, Victoria, Queensland, SA, WA and
Tasmania"

There were several officers in the dug-out. They had just
breakfasted, judging by the pervading aroma of bacon and
fresh bread, although their plates were now clean. Billy
gratefully accepted a mug of sickly sweet stewed tea and
downed the tot of rum in one gulp. Like many of his mates,
he had become quite addicted to the rum ration these days. It
helped to numb his brain, keep his limbs working and take
his mind off the horror.

"Thought you might have a preference for the amber
nectar, being a Jock!" said a marbles-in-the-mouth voice . . .
"Or is it just the bare-arsed kind that drink whisky?"

The officer explained that the heavy lorry was carrying
"accessories" (a code name for gas cylinders) and that they
were urgently needed by a division about five miles away.
Assuming Billy could get the problem solved, he had further
orders to accompany the truck there. He was assigned to the
present company for one week to ensure that a convoy of
trucks got through. Then he would be granted two days
leave. He was to be billetted in a village nearby.

It did not take him long to diagnose the problem. The
lorry simply was not designed for the rough terrain of a shell-
peppered track behind the trenches. The road was full of pot
holes, many flooded with water, and splashing through a
deeper than usual water-logged crater had soaked the engine
and crippled it. Billy dried out the coil, distributor and plugs
and soon had the truck going again. He had to repeat this
procedure many times with the rest of the convoy before the
week was over. A few of the drivers were able to remedy the
fault themselves but the majority were mechanically
incompetent, having been more used to handling horse-
drawn vehicles.

The two days' leave was a pleasant relief, although the
place was dilapidated like all villages in the vicinity of the
trenches. Still, it was refreshing to enjoy a change from the
standard diet of beans with dubious cartilaginous cubes,
masquerading as pork. He managed to secure a meal of soggy
chicken stew and some beer that tasted as if it had been
diluted with canal water, before taking a walk over nearby
fields.

It was a pleasant autumn day. French children peeped
suspiciously from battle-scarred farmhouse doorways, well

warned of passing strangers, but any potential danger was counteracted by childhood curiosity. Billy wanted to talk to them, to join in their play. However, he was no linguist. It would be futile, he decided, so he just smiled and waved at their furtive little faces. Poppies were still blooming like weeds by the roadside and in the meadows. Tough little beauties, he thought, picking one up and flicking a small black fly from the delicate blossom; they even grew defiantly in No-Man's Land, living wreaths to Kitchener's dead army. The first drops of rain hit the petals of the flower as he held it and a distant rumble of thunder heralded another seasonal downpour. Looking around, he saw the ruin of a church. He made for shelter.

It smelt of damp and decay. There was a large shell hole in the roof and part of the far wall was blown away. Neglect and nature had done the rest. He sat down with his back against the remnants of an altar and rummaged through the scattered debris with his hand. Among the wood splinters, broken tiles and rabbits' pirls were some fragments of plaster. He recognised the head and shoulders of a Madonna. He tried to piece it together like a jigsaw but there were not enough bits. Like life itself, he thought. He stared at the battered head, the flaking paint like scars on her face, as if expecting a halo to appear, a divine message to be delivered, but there was only the lashing of the shower on the roof and a drip from the stained glass window where the leaded panel had buckled to the bombs. The rain ran like blood against the vivid red of the glass. Then he heard the creak of the door, hanging lop-sided on its hinges, and a soft muttering:

"Entré, grandpère, asseyez-vous ici."

A bent old man was gently ushered in by a peasant girl. They were still unaware of Billy's presence and he wondered whether to speak. She carried a basket with what looked like berries in it. She took off her shawl and shook it before wrapping it round the old one's shoulders. He seemed fragile, infirm, like a child. She was patient and kind to him.

"Oh, mon Dieu!" she said, catching Billy's slight movement, "Qui êtes-vous . . . ?" She sprang back in a protective gesture, crossing herself and muttering at the same time.

"Eh, A'm sorry, lady, didna mean tae scare dee . . . Eh, A'm English. Weel, Scottish really . . . Écosse."

"Écossais! Mais oui, monsieur, I understand. I speak a little Anglais . . . Are you injured, monsieur?"

"No, just sheltering fae da rain, lik you."

"That is good, monsieur. My name is Michelle. This is André, my grandfather. He does not see now. His eyes are blind. We have been gathering . . . how you say . . . champignons . . . mushrooms?"

"Pleased tae meet you," he said, rising, "A'm Billy." They shook hands.

She was an attractive girl, with reddish brown hair to her shoulders and mahogany coloured skin. Her almond shaped eyes looked straight into his and the directness of her stare both impressed and disconcerted him. She was certainly not shy. She had full hips and a wide sensual mouth. She was dressed simply in a greyish green cotton frock, with a tight bodice, and a lowish neckline revealed the curve of her breasts. Wet warmth seemed to rise from her as he drank in her aesthetically pleasing shapes. She was aware of his ogling and he was sure that she read his thoughts, so he turned his head away in shame.

"Looks lik hit's on for a while?" he said.

"Oui, monsieur, but the sky is clear over there," she said, pointing west through the damaged roof, "It will pass soon." She smiled and he noticed that one of her front teeth was chipped.

"You have cigarettes for grandpapa?" she said.

He fumbled in his pocket and felt the familiar crumpled photograph that he always carried, the one taken at Ramsay's in Lerwick, himself and Peter, Babs . . . and Jean. He wished that he'd made more effort to see her . . . or to write.

He handed Michelle a packet of Woodbines and a box of Vestas. He did not smoke himself but the troops got free cigarette rations and he always carried some for barter or to comfort a wounded mate.

"Merci, monsieur." wheezed the old man, as the girl lit one and placed it between his parchment lips.

"Dix minutes, grandpère," she said. She wandered to the far side of the altar, beckoning to Billy.

"You like a nice time, monsieur?" she whispered, stroking her breast as she did so. "Michelle will give you sweet kisses?"

Billy gazed at her in sheer disbelief . . . She was offering herself . . . She was a whore. She was so young and ordinary . . . pretty, not like the brazen, painted creatures from the "Blue Lamp".

"I . . . I dinna think so, Michelle," he said. His face was flushing and an involuntary pain had crept into his testicles. He tried hard to banish unwholesome thoughts and to concentrate on homely brönnie-baking ones. It didn't work.

"Do not be shy, Billy, it will be all right." She spoke soothingly, seductively, touching his shoulder and leaning towards him so that her breath slid past the side of his ear into the nape of his neck, warm and sweet as honey.

He felt awkward, not knowing whether to push her away and run, or surrender to the throb in his loins. He hesitated too long . . . his hot face and his tented trousers petrified him. He was stiff with desire and apprehension, tinged with disgust at himself.

She took his hand and put it on her breast. It was soft and warm and smelt of olive oil and cut grass. She nibbled his neck and the lobe of his ear and slithered around him like a gentle python, her pelvis grinding against his. I am being seduced, he thought. How crazy . . . incredible . . . how bloody wonderful! He held her now and kissed her urgently and she had him in the palm of her hand.

Then she held him at arms' length and said: "You have ten francs, monsieur?"

"Yes, yes." He was impatient. He pulled her close. The bilious queasiness in the pit of his stomach was now totally dispersed, burnt away forever in an expert kindling of primeval sexuality. He felt dizzy with the warmth of her, intoxicated with the infinitely feminine smell, the taste of her sweet saliva. She opened her mouth to his probing tongue, magnetically drawing throbbing masculine flesh to the hottest part of her body.

CHAPTER
11
Missing

As he walked back to the village, the war-strewn countryside seemed even more bedraggled after the rain. Several horses stood in an immobile sodden group, each with one hind leg raised, reminding him of shelties and home. He chastised himself. He had acted like an animal, not a man . . . but then every man in this lousy war was no better than a beast. Still, now he would not die without having known something of the delights that lay in that deep dark secret world of sex. Michelle knew what she was about all right. She had led him like a child through the gate of discovery, guiding his hands to all her silken places, expertly harnessing his basic instincts till his vigour was spent. It had been a great relief, like lancing a boil. Surprisingly, it was Jean Watt that he'd felt in his arms.

He knew he would seek out this experience again. He would not queue at a whorehouse door and race against the clock and swap stories with his mates but he would go again to Michelle. She had drawn him a simple sketch-map in the dust. "One kilometre" she had said, marking out a neighbouring farmhouse.

"I give you special rate. You are a nice boy, you will bring cigarette and whisky."

Now, he fully understood how whores grew rich serving regiments. He did visit Michelle again, but only once.

At the end of September, he was assigned to the 4th Battalion, Royal Tank Corp, to investigate a fault in the new gear system of a prototype "Devil", a Mark V tank with a purpose-built Ricardo engine, four Hotchkiss machine guns and a unique system of brakes. He fixed it and admired this sophisticated killer, with the ingenious caterpiller tracks instead of wheels. He'd never seen anything so formidable before.

Since the Germans were being particularly active on that stretch of front, a veteran corporal from the 4th Battalion was assigned to escort Billy on a safe exit route back to base.

They were travelling at night for maximum cover when the road in front of them was floodlit with a blinding flare. The earth beneath their feet shook as a loud explosion threw mud and metal everywhere. The corporal fell and groaned. Billy was flung to the ground and managed to crawl into a crater. After several minutes of silence, he assumed it was an isolated bomb and crept towards his companion. A second shell smashed into the hole that he had just vacated, hurling him effortlessly into the air, like a rag. The blackness swallowed him. He felt no pain.

At his unit, the roll-call showed that he was not present over a period of two weeks. Army form B 104-83 was sent to Dr. William Leask in Whiteness, Shetland, notifying his next-of-kin that he was missing in action.

A fortnight later, Army form B 104-82A was also despatched, ending all hope. It said:

". . . *no further news has been received and we are regretfully constrained to conclude that William Leask is dead*".

CHAPTER
12
Willa

"The Big Hoose" in Whiteness was home to Dr. William Leask and one of the rooms acted as his surgery. He had been a parish doctor and public vaccinator, serving part of the West Mainland for over twenty years. Agnes, his wife, hailed from a well-to-do merchant's family. Two sons, Billy (for the past three months missing in action) and James (aged seventeen) and a daughter Margaret (fifteen), completed the household.

They were diverse characters. William Leask, or "Peerie Willie" as he was called in the parish, was a gentle man who loved music and literature and had risen, through learning and opportunity, from humble beginnings. He was of true Shetlandic pedigree, unlike many of his fellow parish doctors, who tended to be imported from the mainland. Few Shetlanders had obtained the means to a medical profession, but he was an exceptional man. He had always been a bright pupil as a child, showing great mechanical and scientific aptitude, interested in chemistry and materia medica.

His fascination with science had started to develop as a toddler when he'd watched his aunt Willa dying wool. She had shown him how to extract the yellow colour from docken root, reddish brown from "old man's beard", orange and purple from two different lichens. Also, from a very young age, he had shown a great interest in treating ailing birds and wild animals by administering pharmaceutical cures and setting broken limbs with plaster of Paris and wooden splints. As a teenager, he had achieved a considerable measure of success and was encouraged by his father to follow his natural vocation. His family had not been well off but they had been bequeathed a little money from an uncle, lost at the whaling, and had invested this inheritance in Willie's education. He had got through the matriculation tests with ease and had done credit to the privilege bestowed upon him by passing several subsequent examinations with merit at Marischal College, University of Aberdeen.

Willie had a well developed sense of humour, much

needed in his work. He was thoroughly liked and respected by all who knew him. He enjoyed an occasional dram or two and he thrived on company. He was an unassuming master of the written and spoken word, not only in his native Shetlandic, but also in Norwegian, Faroese and Icelandic. Consequently, he was frequently called upon to speak at social and official functions.

Agnes, on the other hand, was rather reserved. She seemed an unlikely match for his outgoing personality. She did not care much to socialise at all, and frowned upon senseless frivolity. She had been born and brought up in Lerwick, where her parents and sister, Margaret, still lived. She felt superior to the surrounding crofting women, strong and secure in the knowledge that she was the doctor's wife. Unknown to her, she was described in the district as "the snippet wife fae the big hoose."

The boys looked similar, but this strong family resemblance applied to appearance only. Their personalities were very different. Billy, who would have been twenty years old had he not been lost in action, had been fun-loving like his father, but headstrong, impulsive and troublesome; while Jimmy was a quiet, sickly child who loved to read and hated all crofting activities. Margaret also bore a strong physical likeness to the paternal side, but took after her mother in character. She was a prim and proper girl, with never a hair out of place or a thought out of line.

While the war raged, Jimmy avidly read the daily papers, reporting articles of interest to the others after supper each night. Now, it was January 1919, the war was over, but the local newspapers were still full of recent events at sea, in France, in Palestine, etc. Every Shetland district had lost men and it was an unwelcome part of Willie Leask's duties to attend the wounded and to comfort the bereaved.

He had lived on the West side all his life and he had numerous relatives scattered around the parish of Whiteness. His aunt Willa was his favourite. The old lady lived alone now, was something in excess of the usual threescore years and ten, an eccentric character who spoke her mind and devil take the consequences. She had a few acres of croftland in South Whiteness, near the knowe of Hallibrig. Willie had persuaded Agnes to help her to make full use of it during the thin times of national rationing.

Agnes had taken badly to having to help with sheep and chickens and potatoes and she did not care much for the "kjnittery old wife." However, she had forced herself, under the extreme circumstances, to play a role in her husband's desire for semi-self-sufficiency. (If the truth be told, the restrictions of the food coupons irritated her and she was willing to sacrifice a little hard work and dignity to have a fresh-egg advantage over her sister, who was always bragging about how she had managed to obtain certain scarce or even luxury foodstuffs. One-upwomanship was a family trait).

Willie had lately been suffering from lack of sleep. He felt exhausted all the time. Tuberculosis was rife in his practice and several children had died. He hated to see the disease claim the lives of the young and innocent; neither did he like the stigma attached to these unfortunate families by neighbours, yet he understood that it was born of fear. How often had he heard folk saying to their children "Bide oot o' yun hoose, dir's consumption in yun fok!" Recently, it had become known as the "galloping consumption."

He looked forward to the future, to more enlightened times, when the rudimentary facts about these diseases would be taught alongside English and Arithmetic in the schools. Youngsters would then become aware that these were not hereditary diseases and might begin to appreciate the benefits of simple prophylactic measures like fresh air, sunshine, disinfection and ventilation in their dark overcrowded houses. They might even be encouraged to break the vicious circle by destroying the traditional vile conditions which were an ideal culture ground for the T.B. bacillus. In the meantime, Willie did his best to explain the need to isolate and burn the sputa of their affected near and dear ones and to keep their personal cutlery and crockery away from the asymptomatic members of their family.

He shared the parental grief following the loss of a little one after weeks of dedicated nursing. These days, the sorrow was often compounded by the dreaded telegram telling them that an older child was missing, presumed dead. He himself had never lost hope that Billy might be alive somewhere and he had the rare gift of being able to transfer this hope to other stricken families. Times were hard. Fate had dealt an uneven hand to some poor folk.

Few of the ordinary crofters could afford to pay the statutory call out fee for his services, so he took payment only where he thought it could be spared. He visited many of the impoverished patients free of charge, disguising the

76

consultation as a social visit. His unselfish nature did not go unnoticed because he was rich in friends and had a drawer full of worsted socks, representing thousands of grateful stitches knitted by penniless but willing fingers. Willie had more than his fair share of kindness. For his patients, he had a knack of divining some light even in the bleakest of circumstances. However, at the moment he was unusually lethargic, even though the newly acquired Model T Ford motor car (a bit of a novelty among the horse drawn vehicles) was a godsend and had already speeded up his rounds. He still had to walk many miles to some isolated dwellings, his route often obstructed by mulish, non-functional gates, tied together by pieces of string and designed to dislocate shoulders and generate hernias. He had developed an irrational hatred of rural gates.

He had two calls to make that morning before dropping in on Willa, as he always did on a Friday, just to satisfy himself that the sweetly cantankerous old lady was still to the fore. Firstly he went to see Mansie and Bella Leask and was glad to see that little Beth was recovering. Her fever had peaked and she was up, eating gruel.

The next call was to the Hunter family where he found a less happy state of affairs. Kirsty and Ertie were in their early forties although the former looked well over fifty. She was thin and drawn, with a pallid complexion, the stuffing having been wrenched out of her by the wear and tear of seven children and the subsequent series of disastrous events that had befallen her family. Annie, eight years old, had lost part of her foot when she jumped into a shallow marsh while playing a game near the school. Her innocent bare foot had landed heavily on an old rusty scythe blade, hidden beneath the moss. On that particular day Willie had been attending a patient some distance away and could not be reached quickly. Ertie had attempted to cauterise the wound and stem the considerable blood loss. When Willie eventually reached the scene, she was in terrible pain and in a state of deep shock. He had given her a hypodermic of morphia and dressed the wound every second day thereafter. Ever since then, the girl walked with a pronounced limp and a staff.

The second eldest son, aged nineteen, had been killed in action in France in 1915, and the eldest, George, had come home shell shocked just after Christmas, and developed flu. He was holding on but was still desperately ill. It was a strange virulent kind of influenza and Willie had not seen its like before. He had heard of isolated cases in other parishes and it was rife in Lerwick. He feared an epidemic. Already it had the nickname of the "black flu". Some said that it had originated in the trenches from rats that had fed on human corpses.

Ertie had taken these misfortunes badly: he had become withdrawn and acted strangely, obsessed with cleanliness and fearing contamination from ordinary harmless objects. He was often seen carrying a kishie of peats or some driftwood with his arms fully outstretched and laying the burden down to wash his hands frantically in the burn before going on. He muttered constantly to himself and even washed his hands after touching the sneck of the barn door. He was a sorry case these days and the brunt of the croftwork fell on Kirsty.

Last time Willie had visited, he had advised her to clear the barn and move one of the box-beds in there for the five children, or at least for the three little ones. Keep them away from George, he had said, and there was nowhere else for the mites to go. There was little doubt that this unusual strain of flu had arrived with the survivors of the war. Whatever its evil origin, there was little resistance to it among the indigenous Shetlanders, the young and physically weak being especially in danger. It was touch and go whether George would pull through. He had been hallucinating badly and was semi-conscious much of the time. What irony – to get home safe from the foul battlefields, to fall victim to a stinking illness! Furthermore, if he survived, he might have to suffer the lifelong guilt of having infected and killed a sibling child. God forbid.

Willie was met at the briggiestanes by a dirty faced little ragamuffin who was chasing a scrawny runt of a chicken. It was difficult to identify the child as a girl, so well happit she was in layers of jumpers, old breeks with bare knees, rivlins with the toes out of them, and an oversized woollen bonnet pulled over her skull to the eyebrows so that she had to tilt her whole head backwards to view the visitor. She had an involuntary snotty nose, which she wiped on her sleeve before peering at Willie.

"Shö's laid anither egg i' my bed, Dr. Leask," she said. "We're sleepin oot i' the barn noo, and Hentilaggets his been sleepin dere tö!" A moth-eaten moggy rubbed up against the girl's legs. The tattered cat lived up to her name, looking

78

exactly like a bundle of the discarded strands of old wool that get deposited on fences. Hentilaggets shot off, tail between her legs, as Willie spoke: "Yes, Ruth, and hoo's your bridder da day?"

"He's muckle da sam, Dr Leask, he roars awful trow da night . . . but me mam is no been weel dis last twa days."

Willie's heart sank. He hurried inside. The smell of boiling potatoes mingling with the unmistakable nauseating odour of the sickroom made him surreptitiously pull a camphor impregnated handkerchief out of his pocket and hold it to his nose for a second, quickly stuffing it back in his pocket before Kirsty came into view. She came shuffling through from the ben end and he could see that she was ghost grey and had dark lines under her sunken eyes. On examination, he was relieved to find no trace of fever and no swollen glands in the neck. She had been sick for two days now. She thought that it was something that she'd eaten:

"I'm tried da pills and da syrop that me sister brought but hit did me nae good ava. Den, just yesterday, Mimie o' Breck cam by wi' blood mixture 'at she sent aff fur oot o' da paper . . . and I do feel da better o' it." She pointed towards a little hoard of boxes and bottles on the brace. Willie reached up under a motley assortment of damp children's clothes drying on the raep and withdrew a few of them, wiping off a thin layer of fine peat ash and reading the labels:

"Beecham's pills - for heartburn and low spirits in women; Mother Seigal's syrup – indigestion, headaches, acidity; the familiar box of Doan's backache kidney pills, with the picture of the stereotyped grandmother wagging her finger and saying . . . Take regular dozes of common sense, use medicine only for needed repairs . . .; Keatings – kills bugs, fleas, moths, beetles; Clark's blood mixture – for the blood is life – for blood and skin disorders."

He put them back. Well known, pithless remedies. Still they'd do no harm, and it was certainly better than the witchdoctor home cures of the previous generation, sheep's pirls and milk, and other vile nostrums, ugh!

"Weel, Kirsty, I'll no prescribe ony mair fur dee eenoo. I'll hae a look in at George and leave anither bottle o' yun medicine. It'll help his breathin an settle him a peerie bit trow da night. Try tae git sleep deesel noo." His words lacked conviction.

"Bliss you, bliss you, Willie. What wid we do athoot you. But will you no bide and hae a scar o' tae?"

79

"No dis time, Kirsty. I'm awa tae see wir Willa."

Willa was hale and hearty and had been out feeding her twartree ducks. She had on a pair of ex-serviceman's tackety boots that she'd acquired from an unknown source, with marlin worsted socks on the outside to stop her slipping. It was frosty but most of the snow that had lingered since before Christmas had melted now. She wore two woollen haps on top of a heavy skirt and jumper and an apron, which once boasted a bold pattern but now shone glistening black. She had a dreep on the end of her nose and the shawls were held in place round her ample middle by a piece of string.

"Cum du awa in, Willie. I'm blyde tae see dee but, feth, du's lookin awful little wirt da day, boy . . . Is yun sherger o' a wife o' dine fantin dee aatagidder?"

"Wheest, Willa. Agnes is aa right whin you tak time tae git tae ken her. Shö's no really as trumsket as du maks her oot tae be. Noo, what's du been up tae da day?

"Weel, A'm been furt as far as da hill dyke but hit's takin me aa me time. A'm a bit henkel trams i' dis frost, an A'm faa'n on me erse and clertit mysel wi' gutter. Hit wis aa da faat o' yun hoostak sloo o' a wife fae Strom!"

He laughed. "Du's no been fechtin wi' Maggie Ellen ower da sheep again, is du?"

"Man, shö's just an etterkap . . . but shö god hemm very dritten-lik efter I telt her whit tae do wi' her almark yowe!"

Maggie Ellen Johnston and Willa Leask were renowned as a pair of scrapping auld hens. Nevertheless, they did each other the world of good. Each one charged the other with energy and their respective well-being was directly proportional to the intensity of their rows. Willie knew that under his aunt's stern exterior beat a sincere heart. She would never see her sparring partner wanting for anything if she was ill. It was only last hairst that she'd walked to Strom with a pot o' broth when Maggie was laid up with pains in the kidneys and booel-cramps.

"Noo, will du hae a scar o' tae, jewel? A'm just awa tae bake. Du'll maybe haand me doon me bakin mittens?"

"I'll tak a cup o' tae, Willa, but nae bread. A'm been kinda aff me maet lately. I'm a bit döless."

He reached towards a hook above the stove where the familiar pair of unsavoury mittens hung, knitted woollen remnants, cemented and starched by years of successive baking sessions. They smelt distinctly of rancid dripping and tiny, caked balls of stale flour and dough adorned their palmar surface. The odd brave worsted hair still managed to protrude through this armour cladding.

Willa swore by them and she did bake a fine brönnie. To her, this was the height of hygiene. " Yun lipper fae Strom cleans her sharny hands in her bakin dough, fur A'm seen her wi' me ain eyes!" she had said, last time he had challenged her sacred baking accessories. The heat generated by the cooking would likely kill a multitude of germs, he reassured himself.

After his tea and a soul-regenerating yarn, he headed back towards the big hoose. He had a surgery that afternoon although he would have liked better to go to his bed and sleep for a week. The patient clinics were always eventful since the people who attended usually included a few relatively well heeled notables, some with hypochondriac tendencies. Jessie Morrison, for instance, was thought to have demonic powers and went around muttering to herself all the time. This fierce old witch demanded medicines for imaginary complaints. Lately, he had satisfied her with a unique tonic mixture, made from cold tea, cloves, a few drops of gentian violet for colour and a generous measure of whisky. Jessie liked this placebo (which was prescribed in strict moderation) and claimed great bodily benefits.

Other characters carried their own containers for "some o' yun sam stuff du gied me twa year ago". The bottles that they brought were usually oversized and dirty, frequently laced with the dismembered remains of a long-legged spider floating in dregs of brown liquid. After many failed attempts at teaching them the rudiments of semi-aseptic technique, he had given up. Instead he now encouraged Agnes to keep a small varied supply of sterile bottles for cod liver oil, eye drops and other potions and ointments which he dispensed himself. Of course these patients were but an eccentric few. There were many deserving folk with genuine troubles.

At home, a letter awaited him. It had an English postmark and he recognised the seal of the Royal Engineers. He opened it:

"Dear Dr. Leask,

I am writing to inform you that your son, William Leask, has just been transferred to this military hospital as a patient. He has been sent here from No. 8 Red Cross Hospital in Rouen, France, where he has been treated for several injuries over the past few months. Since his identity papers were missing and he was wounded while on temporary duty as a sapper attached to another division, it was some time before we were able to communicate with him and so establish the whereabouts of his next of kin.

At present, he is recovering from a compound fracture of the right femur, which is extremely slow to heal, and he has lost two fingers on his right hand. Also, he has had shrapnel lodged in his throat and has barely audible speech, although we hope that this will improve.

In addition to these physical injuries, he has classic symptoms of shell shock and, taking all these ailments into consideration, it may be several months before he is fit to travel.

He is otherwise stable and responding well to treatment. We will endeavour to keep you informed of his progress.

Yours sincerely,

Dr. J. H. Mawdsley."

Willie's eyes filled with tears and then he was leaping around like a new slippit calf, shouting "Agnes! Agnes! He's alive! Billy is alive!" His ample heart was full to bursting point.

CHAPTER

13

The Calm after the Storm

"From Bulgaria's humble submission, September 29th, 1918, the central powers tumbled like a house of cards. November 9th saw the red flag waving over Berlin and the imperial Kaiser a hunted refugee, fleeing for the Dutch border."
Extract from the war news, Shetland Times,
January 1919

The UK statistics indicated that 9% of all men under 55 had been lost and there were 1.6 million gravely wounded. In Shetland 35% of the total male population had served in the war and over 600 men never came back. Widowed and single women with young children were plentiful in Lerwick.

John Watt served as a chief petty officer on board H.M.D. "Felicia" and was lost at sea on July 2 1917, when his vessel was torpedoed. He was forty-two years old and left behind his wife Mary and four children. The family was devastated by the loss but strangely united with the Shetland community in a new and stronger way, by mutual grief. Men had been lost everywhere and were in short supply. War, like poverty, is a great equalizer.

Johnie, in particular, took the death of his father badly. He was thirteen when the news came, an impressionable age, and the remaining year of the war coincided with his awkward adolescence. He became progressively quieter and even more withdrawn, a different person. He played truant from school and was not missed, because so many of the Scottie children were kept home to help with chores. His antisocial behaviour was a constant source of worry to the family. Jean tried to reach him but he remained silent in his shell. He was full of a deep-rooted bias against all authority. Although seldom openly cheeky, he treated all forms of officialdom with dumb insolence and went his own secretive way. He played practical tricks on people, like putting a hedgehog in Elsie's bed and covering the chimney with a damp mossy peat to smoke out the household. He burnt the cat's whiskers off with matches, leaving only frizzled knobs on short stalks. The cat was terrified of him after that. He spent hours alone, wandering in and out of the house at odd times.

James West, gunner, R.N.R.,ss "Glenlea" returned to Shetland in December 1918. The fighting on the Russian northern front was still in full swing and many of the troops were retained for transport and for the administration of civilian duties. However, James had been wounded and arrived complete with a slight limp in his right leg and a silver tipped walking stick, deliberately chosen in the hope that the classy stick would somehow minimise his disability! His once gentle nature had been hardened by the trauma of these years.

James had briefly seen Jean in 1916, when she was ill, and twice more during his home leave. He had courted her with a quiet, old-fashioned dignity, bringing material presents and smiles, although few words. He hadn't touched her. He did not think it right to love and leave as so many of his contemporaries had done. It was a ruthless time and he could not bear to get too close to a woman and maybe never come back. Nevertheless, these weary years had brought the values most important in his life into sharp focus: he was more determined than ever to skipper his own boat and he badly yearned for a home with a loving wife and family. Surely this was what he had fought for, he reflected.

The Mission now had dedicated staff but he would continue to volunteer his services on an occasional basis.

He resolved to pick up the threads of courtship. Once back home, one of his first duties was to visit the Watt household and pay his respects to Mary and Jean, offering his sincere sympathy on the sad loss of a husband and father who had been his friend.

Jean was also weary. She too was seeking security. She missed her father; she had felt the inner foreboding for a full fortnight before the telegram came, as had her grandmother, although neither of them had worried Mary at the time. Jean had heard so many tales of grief. She had seen for herself so many gallant young men maimed and dying. She had witnessed the agonies of the widows and children. She remained sick at heart with the terrible reports of war, such as the news that the Czar of Russia had been murdered by his Bolshevik captors and that the Czarina and Princesses were foully done to death in their prison. She had always believed in God Almighty. However, disillusionment had set in lately and her faith had grown weaker. Consequently, her tenuous relationship with James West developed quickly. The extreme social, financial, and personal pressures of the time catalysed their courtship and provided the exact formula for a whirlwind romance.

They saw the old year out and a new one in. They heard the Town Hall clock striking midnight and watched the yellow glow from the heartwarming handful of gas lamps lighting the streets after years of depressing blackout. She held his hand. She felt very proud and safe holding on to this gentle giant of a man, who had surely survived the war and sought her company through fate. She was reminded of that Sabbath evening in Crovie, so long ago, when she held her father's rough hand and heard the unspoken communication from his soul. She knew, beyond doubt, that she would marry James West. She was equally sure that he would ask her soon. Yet her sixth sense warned of a dark trouble lurking.

She shivered and wilfully banished this inauspicious sensation. No superstitious nonsense would spoil her happiness. Then her Hogmanay fears were interrupted by the celebrating whistles of the vessels in the harbour piercing the crisp icy air and the cheers of the guizers milling around the Market Cross, heralding the first complete year of peace and tranquillity after a long time of conflict.

"Happy New Year, Jeanie," he said, kissing her and filling her heart with longing.

They did not talk of the terrible hardships. They did not allow themselves to worry about the galloping consumption and the black flu that swept through their town in the wake of the war. They wanted to wash it all away and start afresh, with each other, to enjoy the calm after the storm. Newspapers were still full of residual bad news such as the leave ship that ran aground at full speed, near Stornoway, and left 200 recently discharged war veterans washed up dead on their native beaches.

Things were changing rapidly all through the country: there had been a coalition victory and Mr. Asquith was rejected. The growing actions of the suffragettes were winning ground on the issue of female equality. The new government promised better times to come. She and her man would be ready and united to go with the wind and sail on a tide of change.

James had saved a little money but he needed a loan to

raise enough capital to buy a boat. Since he had no collateral, he decided not to approach a bank but to visit Silas Smith, a backstreet moneylender, operating his lucrative business from premises selling second-hand clothes.

The shop was dark and dingy, smelling of perished rubber, mothballs and dust. A sallow-faced youth stood behind the counter, head bent over a ledger in pensive silence. He was neatly dressed in a worn dark jacket, collar and tie. He raised his head from his work but offered no greeting, merely staring at James with a blank expression. His face reminded James of a sooked piltock.

"I'd like t' see Mr. Silas Smith, if he's available," James prompted the immobile assistant.

"Eh . . . My father's in the office at the back mister. Through there." He pointed to a narrow passage behind the counter, stacks of clothing lining either side.

The moneylender was a short, balding man, with a complexion much like his son's, clearly an indoor creature. He wore a well tailored suit, a gold watch chain dangled from a waistcoat pocket and pince-nez spectacles were perched perilously on the end of his nose. He was forcibly polite although his curt manner made it clear that he was reluctant to assist.

"So you have no collateral, Mr . . . West, did you say? . . . and you cannot give me a recorded history of your past catches . . . I have only a small business, Mr. West. I must be careful to choose reliable clients. It is not possible to agree such a loan to a complete stranger."

"I understand, Mr. Smith, I'm sorry I've wasted yer time . . . and m' ain . . . by coming here."

Silas pulled out his watch as if to emphasise that his time was valuable.

"Harold! . . . show this man out," he called.

The youth scuttled through the clothes canyon. As he held the office door open, his pock-marked face creased into an artificial smile, revealing uneven, discoloured teeth. James had to squeeze past him, getting a whiff of breath that smelt of rancid butter and strong mutton. As he left the premises, he heard Silas mutter: "Don't you show any more Scotties through here, boy. I won't be doing business with fishermen."

"But father..."

"Don't answer back, boy! Now, run along home and ask your mother to put the tatties on."

"Yes father."

James felt humiliated and angry. What a bloody cheek! A record of catches indeed... did the man not realise he'd been on active service? He decided to treat the incident with the contempt it deserved and not to mention it to anybody.

He joined forces with two other men to purchase a forty foot fishing boat, as equal shareholders. She was fifteen years old and going at a bargain price. A dual purpose vessel, she would fish for haddock in the winter and herring in the summer. She was fully decked, with a five-man cabin, and would require a conversion; the Fishery Board and the Zetland County Council were actually considering the practicality of providing a loan scheme to allow the installation of modern diesel engines.

Jean managed to get a counter position with the local firm of John W. Robertson, Brown's Buildings, providing supplies for boats, fishcuring requisites, agricultural items like seeds and scythes, and a range of stoves for heating and cooking. The wages were poor and she knew she could make more at the herring gutting, but the season might be slow to start this year and she gratefully accepted the job as a stopgap until the Springtime. She needed every penny she could earn to help James set up with the boat. Ordinary foodstuffs had gone up enormously during the war years: milk by 50%; butter 75%; loaf 250%; and sugar over 300%.

Mary, her mother, now received a small widow's pension, 7/6d per week, so her family were not destitute although they were far from well off. Mary had developed a nervous disposition, worrying excessively about her elder son. Jean persuaded James to take the melancholy, withdrawn Johnie on as a loon aboard the "Prosperity", the name he had chosen for his new investment. He was none too keen on the idea, however, since he worried that the boy's antisocial behaviour might affect his crew and bring bad luck. On the other hand, he recognised his extended family responsibility and wanted to please Jean. Perhaps hard work and company would bring this peculiar boy out of himself. He would give him 5/- a week plus his provisions on board, for a trial period anyway.

The harbour remained a busy place. Lerwick was designated an intermediate base for British operations in Northern Russia. There was a steady trickle of troop and cargo vessels as Archangel and Murmansk were evacuated. Lerwick was also earmarked as a base for United States minesweepers and "The Knights of Columbus", a social organisation, entered the post-war spirit with typical

American panache, organising dances and boxing tournaments in the Rechabite Hall. British links with the States grew strong. In the words of Winston Churchill: "Britain's reward for her part in this war for justice and humanity is the birth of a new unity for the two great English-speaking nations."

American influence was everywhere. Jean thought that James might propose the night he took her to the North Star Cinema to see a film called "The Honeymoon", starring Constance Talmadge. It was a thought-provoking film, set against the wonderful romantic background of Niagara Falls. There was such an endearing little dog too, and the plot hinged on the Yankee attitude to easy divorce and matrimonial misdemeanours, with sexual undertones that made Jean blush and burn. She was beginning to feel the tension as James persevered in his personal struggle to overcome shyness and pop the question.

Perhaps it was the unfortunate incidents with Gideon that delayed his proposal. The preacher burst into the cinema twice during the evening shouting "Bide oot o' this hoose o' evil! Look not at the devil's images!" Poor Gideon. Since the war, he'd tried even harder to impose his own interpretation of God's will on the whole community.

The following Friday at the Rechabite Hall, James did propose. He had help from a little bit of Dutch courage, being mildly inebriated, just enough to overcome his inhibitions. The dance was well attended and jolly. Jean looked radiant, her ash blonde hair in loose curls down her back and little side combs holding it behind her ears. She liked her hair loose, since she had never quite recovered from the tight pigtails and bunches inflicted by her mother when she was younger: sometimes the ribbons had been put in so tight that her skin was pulled taut, making her eyes slant so that she looked oriental. Her pale blue dress had a lowish neckline and a small bustle at the back. It rustled as she walked and she felt very grand.

As they passed by the big mirror in the hall, she caught sight of their reflection together. They made a handsome couple. They were attempting to dance a waltz to the music of Ronnie Mathewson (piano) and Private J. Cluness (violin). James's injured leg was only the mildest of handicaps and his natural rhythm was easy to follow. He was as comfortable to be with, to dance with, . . . to marry, as an old armchair, she thought. She accepted without hesitation.

They laughed aloud and danced with renewed energy, their hearts joyful.

They married on 20th January, 1919. The wedding was a quiet affair, a simple church service followed by a small family celebration at home. Jean made her own dress, a plain cream satin with heavy piping and large buttons covered in bright green and blue checks. Her grandmother had objected to the dazzling buttons because "Blue and green should never be seen..." Still, she had approved of the finished effect and had lent Jean her own little fox fur for the occasion. They walked to and from the service. The only luxury was their wedding cake. It had been ordered by Mary, but only after Elsie had cut an advertisement out of the newspaper and left it lying around the house as a gentle hint, along with her own ration coupons. The advertisement read:

"Malcolmson & Company,
Marriage cakes our speciality,
Made on the shortest notice,
iced plain or according to order."

It seemed that Mary needed broad hints these days: she had become rather absent-minded and was always preoccupied. It was her way of coping with her grief and her son Johnie's sullen behaviour. Once a sweet lovable child, he was a stranger to the family now, always engaged in solitary pursuits and with erratic sleeping patterns, frequently shutting himself in the shed for hours on end. He was much troubled within himself and had refused to go to church after his father died. Still, James said that he was becoming a good worker on board the boat and Jean decided he was just going through a difficult patch.

The family clubbed the rest of their ration coupons together to ensure a decent spread for the small gathering of friends and relatives. Meat, sugar, butter and margarine were still rationed, although at least the margarine allocation had increased from two to five ounces per person.

The war was behind them. Anticipation of married life, and all that it entailed, was sweet.

CHAPTER
14
Jekyll and Hyde

Something snapped. He crept quietly out of the warm bed into the early dawn. He liked the twilight. Mr Hyde had taken over and a queer light gleamed in his altered eyes. The twisted recesses of his mind brimmed with unmentionable thoughts and warped desires.

He had a large hook firmly embedded in the throat of the fish as he threw it high into the air amidst the squawking gulls. It was swallowed before it hit the ground and, as the unfortunate gull flew off, the hook stuck in its throat and a line ran from the hook to his sweaty hand. He felt a fine tremor of excitement and satisfaction as it tensed.

He giggled. He pulled in the string with the flapping captive trying in vain to regurgitate the deadly bait. He liked to hurt things. His spine tingled and he danced around the scruffy patch of weed-ridden grass, acting like a kitten playfully enjoying the death throes of a tortured mouse. He felt powerful, just as he had felt when he had wrung the necks of a nest of baby starlings that he had clawed from a hole in a wall, or when he filled a fish with rusty nails before throwing it to a gull flying over water and watched with fascination the desperate sinking and drowning of the victim. But . . . wait . . . What was that noise? Footsteps were approaching.

"Ssh, somebody coming! Ssh, hide . . . good boy . . . hide . . . Shh."

He let go of the line, allowing the wounded gull to fly away in torment, trailing the tackle, to die a slow death somewhere else. He hid by the side of an old building and fiddled absent-mindedly with the flaccid flesh of a frog in his pocket. He liked the feel of its slimy cold skin, it reminded him of his own private parts and the warm glow that came when he played with himself. Yesterday had been the last time, as he'd watched the pretty toddler playing alone in the back yard. He had seen her through a hole in the fence . . . and given her a candy bar to pee in his tin can . . . and let him watch her.

He had sprawled on the ground, then, and tilted his head to view the act. He had grabbed the can of hot urine and run off to the garden shed, his own domain, where he indulged his private fantasies and planned his moves. He was brimming with visible, restless energy. He needed to hurt something else, a stray dog... or a helpless squirming child, to feel the pulsing heart thumping in the little chest as it squeaked and whined. What joy! Pleasure! Strength! It made his blood race and his manhood was big in every way. The footsteps passed. His hiding place was secure.

He looked at the sky to get an indication of the time. Nearly seven o'clock . . . many of the workers would be passing soon . . . better head for home. He ambled along the shoreline, skimming flat stones into the water and seeing them skip and hop across the surface before being lost in the depths. The sea can engulf anything, he thought, stone or flesh, dead or alive, swallow them up. He swallowed as if he were the sea. He peeped over the edge of a slipway and caught his reflection in the water . . . a smart image, he thought, sticking out his chin and puffing his chest to improve his watery profile. He headed towards his sanctuary.

He opened the door and entered the dim dusty hovel where he spent so many of his hours, isolated from humanity. It smelt of stale pigswill and cat's piss and was strewn with clutter. It was a comforting familiarity. He licked his slobbery lips with a furred tongue. There was a box containing papers, an old chair with his necktie draped over it, and a table with instruments: his trusty penknife; bent wires; assorted nails; a rusty poker and a broken saw blade. He liked to cut things open to see their innards. Animals were better than cold blooded fish, their twisting turning intestines warm to touch. Perhaps he would set a trap for the next cat that mewed at the door in search of scraps.

"Where are you, sweetheart? You're not out there again, are you? . . . It's time for breakfast." The call came clear and warm on the morning air.

"I'm here . . . in the shed, mother. Coming!" He hurriedly sorted out his secret things so she wouldn't be angry. It was best that she didn't know. She didn't like him hurting things. She'd warned him to stay away from young children, but he liked so much to watch them on the swings. A glimpse of bare thighs and underwear made the sweat sweet on him.

He put away Mr Hyde and assumed an innocent

91

expression and dutifully knotted his tie. His mother might suspect something. She might worry constantly but she was his mother and she would banish these niggling thoughts. He was her son. She loved him. She would help and protect him from the evil within.

CHAPTER
15
Teething Troubles

Jean and James rented two small rooms on the ground floor of a big house in Parkfield Road (now St. Sunniva Street). The building belonged to James's aunt. Flora West was a rather stern old spinster, who looked after her father and was virtually stone deaf. The newly weds did have some privacy, not having to associate with her on a daily basis and having their own door, immediately inside a back entrance that they shared with another family who lodged there. Flora and her elderly father used the front.

The bigger of the rooms served as living space and bedroom. It was clean but cramped, barely sufficient accommodation for their bed and the small chest of drawers with the wooden framed looking-glass. It was Mary's mirror, given to Jean when she moved. It had lovely spiralled ends that reminded Jean of barley sugar sticks, knobs for feet and a small round handle on the front that opened a little drawer for holding her few precious personal things: a comb, a pin brooch that Babs Wiseman had gifted her, two favourite net needles, four mother of pearl buttons cut from an old blouse, her father's watch which she had been given as a keepsake, a photograph of Johnie as a bright smiling youngster, and a flat skimming stone "guaranteed to work, even for a hopeless quinie lik you, Jeanie", Johnie had assured her. She wasn't sure why she kept the silly stone. Perhaps it reminded her of happier days.

Beside the open fireplace stood two worn armchairs, purchased second hand from one of Frank Smith the auctioneer's sales of household furniture in the fish market. Her pride and joy was the present given to them by James's family: a pair of glass domed sidepiece lustrous ornaments, deep blue vases with hand painted flowers, hung with chandeliers, all covered with a domed glass dust cover. They had no functional use but she thought they were beautiful and polished them frequently.

The adjoining scullery was very small, with a black empress stove for cooking, a table, two chairs and a marble

93

top washstand. Everything had to be done in these tiny rooms, including the regular baiting of the haddock lines. There was running water from an outside tap and a shed served as a shared lavatory. Jean took her turn with the other residents to empty the bucket from the lavatory and clean it out with Jeyes fluid. They were fortunate to have an additional small coal shed in the alley leading to the back of the house.

The rooms were draughty and never seemed to get very warm, even when the coal fire was lit and well primed with fuel. Most of the time, however, Jean kept the fire low because the heat made the smell of the bait strong and nauseating. It was preferable to shuffle round the room with three layers of clothing on. She had fallen pregnant straightaway; although unconfirmed, she knew that she was six weeks gone. There was no need to consult the doctor. After all, she was young and healthy and there were better things to waste money on. She was happy about the matter, but already she was suffering badly from morning and evening sickness and she went about shivering for much of the day.

The confined smell of cooking especially made her sick and it was a struggle to shell the mussels and bait the lines between bouts of vomiting. Even a whiff of the tarry twine in the dresser drawer made her ill. Other odours, like turpentine and fertiliser from the shop, were even sharper. In addition to these minor discomforts, she had developed toothache lately, a chronic nagging ache which was worse than the nausea. Her teeth had generally deteriorated since working with the TNT powder.

It was now almost the end of March and James was away early most days, except Sunday. Johnie came for him every morning in the raw hours. They wondered if the boy ever slept at all. A few patches of the snow that fell in January still cluttered the pavements, dirty and black with wear though still stubbornly frozen in the north facing places where the thin winter sunshine never penetrated. The steps at the back were treacherous and Jean had taken home a bag of coarse salt from Robertson's to sprinkle on them and on the footpath.

She woke to the clip-clop of a horse-drawn carriage. It was almost six-thirty a.m. and still pitch dark. However, stirrings in the town had long since begun and a distant clattering could be heard from the general direction of the harbour; the faint happy sound of coopers trussing barrels echoed like the heartbeat of Lerwick. It was a comforting noise, its rhythmic cadences almost forgotten during the war. Soon the seagulls would be screaming their hungry dawn chorus and the pale watery sunshine would struggle through whatever mist and sleet the day might bring.

Jean didn't like the tail end of winter. She especially didn't relish waking up alone this particular morning, with James's side of the bed cold and stiff, the warm body long gone and a frozen condensation glazing the top of the bedclothes. She rolled over, tentatively poking out her hand from under the heavy covers to brush off the damp icy particles. She was reluctant to shift because the sickness would sweep over her as soon as she got up although she had much to do before her work at eight-thirty. Married life, so far, was not very romantic, really. She ran a hand over her swollen right breast, more evidence of the child within her, and pondered on the miracle of life. She loved her man dearly yet the physical side of her marriage had been painful in the beginning and remained disappointing. Perhaps this was normal. Nobody spoke of such things and certainly she could not discuss it with him. He was gentle enough and she wanted to share everything with him and please him so much. Yet, curiously, her sweet anticipation was out of proportion with the act itself: it was not what she expected at all. James was always silent during lovemaking. She longed to hear him speak words of endearment and instruction because he was surely a man of the world and knew such things while she did not. Yet the ease of communication never came. He seemed to have no need of it. He was comfortable in his silence and fulfilled in his desire when he uttered his little moan of climax and lay still. Secretly, she was quite relieved when it was over. It was another chore without pleasure.

The clock on the wall struck quarter to seven and she sat up with a start. She sighed and pulled back the covers, feeling the frigid air penetrate her extremities right away. She rubbed the ice from the inside of the small window pane and looked out. The gas lamps from the main streets were glimmering in the distance and lights flickered from the boats in the harbour, yellow and smeared in morning mist. Male voices shouting anxious instructions of some kind or another rose above the usual cacophony of harbour sounds.

She struck a match to light the stove, already set with

kindlers made from the staves of broken herring barrels, from yesterday's part-burnt ashes and a few lumps of fresh coal. The kettle was filled with water already and she was thankful to her husband for this thoughtful gesture. She poured a dribble of it into the basin to wash her face and left the rest to boil for tea. The smell of carbolic soap set her stomach churning and she held her breath. Without exhaling again, she quickly put her clothes on, folded her night-gown and stowed it under the bolster . . . She gasped for air.

She pulled a clean shift from the overhead wooden pulley, smelling and testing the fabrics against her cheek for dryness as she folded them ready for James. It was difficult to tell if the cold material was really dry and the clothes still emanated a lingering trace of his smell. She rolled the bundle (winceyette shirt, flannel shirt, socks and pinkish woollen drawers) thinking of the appropriate parts of his body as she did so. She'd never seen him naked and wondered what he looked like. She had never even seen him take a bath in the zinc tub: he preferred to go to his mother's once a fortnight for his wash. Perhaps he was sensitive about his injured leg. He'd been spending a lot of time at his mother's recently. She hugged the bundle and put it on the chair nearest the stove. He was a good man. He would be a good father.

The hushed tones of Arthur, her fellow shop assistant, and his two early customers faded into silence as she arrived that morning. They turned to stare. She recognised one of them as Maggie Muckie, a notorious town gossip.

"Hello, Maggie." she said cheerfully. "Foo are you this morning?"

"Fine, thank you, Mrs West . . . but I wis just tellin Arthur and Jemima here the terrible news . . ."

"Oh aye, Maggie, fit news is at noo?"

"Lass, lass, his du no heard . . . dir's been a bairn interfered wi' ida toon! . . . I heard at shö wis only five year old . . . Hit's a terrible thing for her fok."

"A bairn, Maggie, are you sure?"

"Dat am I . . . I wish hit wis a lie but hit's as sure as A'm standing afore dee. The bairn is surely no dat seriously hurted . . . sho just greets a lok trow da night. Lerwick is turned intae a terrible place. We're no even safe tae let wir bairns play i' da street noo." Turning towards her companions she continued ". . . Dir's too mony soothmoothers here if you ask me!"

"Do they have ony idea at aa?" Arthur said. Maggie huddled closer to her cronies, full of the swank that gossips bestow upon themselves:

"Weel . . . dey dinna ken fur sure. Da peerie lass could gie dem nae sense ava . . . but da police are interviewing twartree o' yun queer characters aroond here . . . hit's no afore time too."

"Wha, Maggie?"

"Weel, yun fellow fae aside da Fort, him caa'd Haddie & Chips, his been questioned . . . and he got dat mad at he's packed up his stall and geen! . . . Dir also been aside yun queer preacher and his midder nearly flayed dem! Gideon himsel wis mair moderate . . . he just chanted sections o' da Book . . . aboot turning da idder cheek an tings lik dat . . . he's certainly no right ida head, yun creature."

Three pairs of eyes turned towards Jean but she did not feel like rallying to the defence of her cousin. After all, he was indeed a peculiar man and she had never liked him much . . . but to be responsible for this. No.

"Gideon's nae a child molester, Maggie. He's a bittie eccentric, 'at's aa," she said. She brushed past them and quietly began her chores. She would not give them the satisfaction of discussing the matter further. As she went through to the back, she heard Maggie mutter:

"Yun Scotties are aa queer . . . dey say her ain bridder taks efter Gideon . . ."

Jean ignored them. She engaged her mind with more comforting matters, like her own future with James. During their short courtship she had enjoyed their occasional social outings very much but these luxuries had stopped since the wedding day. He now had the worrying expense of the boat and she knew that it would take them a year or two to establish a fair standard of living. The fishing was off to a poor start. There was no fishmarket in operation yet and it was difficult to get decent prices for the catch. Her own small wage barely covered the rent for their rooms and a few groceries. She did try hard to put a little money aside for emergencies and zealously collected all the family's old clothes for the rag-and-bone man, Peter Mackay from North Roadside, who gave good prices for cotton rags and 5/6 a stone for the woollens. Nevertheless, they saved little. Their one weekly outing nowadays was to the Lerwick Parish Church for the Sunday morning service.

The oil of cloves didn't dull the whining pain of the toothache for more than a few seconds. Jean had applied it with the tiniest piece of cotton wool she could handle, yet the foreign mass still felt enormous in her mouth and the burning bitter taste of the cloves made her retch. There was no alternative, she would have to see a dentist.

She picked up the Shetland Times and searched for the advertisement. It read:

> *"Dentistry,*
> *Mr. J. P. Henderson,*
> *Painless extractions,*
> *Artificial teeth all prices*
> *Ellesmere House,*
> *Hours 10-1 and 3-6."*

She headed for Ellesmere House at the head of Victoria Pier at 10 a.m. sharp next day. In lieu of working extra hours at break times, she was allowed one hour to visit the dentist. She was apprehensive and her tongue fiddled with the sore tooth as she hurried along.

There were three people in the waiting room and she immediately recognised Dr. William Leask. She hesitated, the door still ajar, and felt an overwhelming urge to retreat. A sharp jab from the rotten tooth overrode the sickly nostalgic memory of her previous encounters with this man. He looked up from some document that he was reading and his haunting eyes met her gaze. She looked at the floor, then hurried to the far side of a room that seemed to shrink in size as she did so. His eyes followed her and she felt them boring into her. She had barely sat down when he spoke: "Excuse me, miss, but do I no ken you fae somewye?"

"Oh! . . . I dinna think so, sir." she stammered, a beetroot flush blooming under her collar and seeping into her cheeks and ears.

"Yes, yes, I mind noo. We met one day at Margaret and Ertie Manson's at the Hillhead. You're a freend of wir Billy's..the Watt lass, if I mind right? "

"Aye, sir, My name wis Watt, Jean Watt. It's West noo. I got married earlier 'is year."

"Weel, weel, congratulations are in order den, Jean". He smiled at her and got up. " I never forget a pretty face," he said, as she tentatively shook the proffered hand, ". . . and I'm gled you've found your young man. I mind yun day. I was

98

vexed no tae hiv a chance to spaek tae you and your friend but wir Agnes wis in a mood for flytin. I'm sorry aboot yun silly carry on . . . I really dinna ken whit ails yun women sometimes. You're no tae tink dat we're aa lik dem!"

Willie with his warmth and his blue eyes quickly melted her apprehension. It was a full twenty minutes before he was called to the dental surgery, and the chance encounter passed by in a pleasant and mutually informative interchange of news. She learned of Billy's misfortune, that he had been feared lost until a few weeks ago and remained seriously injured. She was glad that he was alive. She had not thought of him often in the last year but now she could not deny a sense of sweet sadness . . . yet it had been but baby love, five cold years ago.

She noticed herself confiding in this familiar stranger who was easy to talk to and eager to communicate with her, just like his easygoing son. Like father, like son, she thought; so unlike my father and my quiet James . . . and Johnie. Why did people change? They were so complicated. This man, though, he seemed homespun, open. She liked him. She was sorry when he was called.

"Perhaps we'll bump into each idder again," he said. " Goodbye and . . . good luck."

"Cheerio, Dr. Leask. Please be sure to gie my best wishes to Billy."

She felt invigorated, alive. Her toothache seemed negligible. However, it returned with a vengeance when Mr. Henderson prodded it with a metal hook. The extraction was anything but painless. She thought her jaw would break as the pliers wrenched back and forth and the awful crunching and tearing of tissue rendered through her skull.

The hole left by the molar was jelly soft and it tasted of iron. She examined the wounded gum in her mother's mirror, her finger stained and her front teeth streaked red. The sheep and herring blood of her youthful dream she recalled vividly. It make her dizzy. She wondered why. She was happily married to one of her own kind. There was nothing to fear from the gentleman: he was pleasant, kind, intelligent, so . . . unassuming. He had treated her like an equal.

She stared into the mirror, deep in thought. James, who had entered quietly, grabbed her waist and spun her round.

"Give us a smoorikin, quine?" he teased as she shrieked with the shock.

She kissed him lightly and fondly. She laughed, pointing

to his sweater: "Och, Yer gansey's on ootside in again, you daft tattie."

"Oh aye, lass. Weel . . . hit'll ging on the richt wye roond the neest time. Y'ken t'is bad luck tae turn it afore ga'in aff."

She laughed again at yet another of his superstitions. She reached into a pocket and held out the tooth. He nodded, pleased for her, and sat down at the table. She knew that food was now expected, not chitchat. Well fine, she did not need conversation. She loved her strong silent fisherman. She loved his unborn child, active in her womb. The war was over. The toothache was gone. They would survive other teething troubles.

CHAPTER
16
A Glisk i da Winter Mirk

Agnes Leask laid down her pen and read the finished letter:

"   *3 April 1919*
Dearest Son,
We are so pleased to hear from Dr. Mawdsley that you continue to make progress and are recovering from all your wounds. We all look forward to seeing you later in the year. Let me emphasise that you are welcome here at home and I am prepared to start afresh and forget our bygone difficulties. Your father would like to help you to start your own engineering business. He has bought a motor car and thinks it is a great thing. I am still wary of it although I must admit that they are becoming more popular in Lerwick and even in the countryside.
Do as the doctors tell you and stay away from patients with the flu. We are all well here although your father has been tired lately. He has been working too hard, with so many of his patients affected by the black flu and the consumption also all around us. He attended a child at Tingwall yesterday and fears that it could be a case of diphtheria. He has had trouble with his teeth and visited the dentistry in Lerwick last week. While he was there, he bumped into the Watt lass that you used to hang around with. She is married now and expecting a bairn . . ."

Agnes smiled with satisfaction as she read this seemingly innocent statement, knowing that there was no possibility now of a rekindling of the teenage attraction. She had better hopes for Billy. The local merchant's daughter was a fine upstanding girl with a bit of breeding to her credit and her father was well off too. Agnes was determined to see a good match for at least one of her children. Her daughter was becoming a bitter disappointment, choosing to spend her time of late with a coarse and penniless young crofter from Bixter. Still, Margaret was young and might see sense yet.

James, the other son, was still a weak lad with more interest in books than in anything else. He would probably never marry, she thought, so her hopes were pinned on Billy providing the wounds of war would heal and he was still able and willing to charm the opposite sex.

She had become increasingly petty minded during the years of conflict, annoyed particularly at the lack of easily available foodstuffs, resentful of having to get her hands dirty with soil and sheep, and irritated by the ill health prevailing all around her. She wanted to move back to the town where her sister enjoyed a better life-style and access to more social conveniences; and also to escape from people like Willa who really was beyond all reason with her slovenly habits and loose tongue.

She was impatient with everyone and everything these days. Her heart had turned sour and she seemed to cast a shadow on the lives within her orbit. The kinder side of her nature had withered and become as paper thin as the walnut veneer on her dressing table.

Willie lived in that grey shadow. His warm character continued to thrive despite his wife's gloomy personality. He remained resilient and resourceful, finding joy in everyday things, in many of his patients, his children, his surroundings . . . and his poetry. Yet, lately, he had begun to feel weary as if he were carrying a burden that was heavier than usual.

The fatique became worse until, after a typical day of physically and emotionally draining work, he needed to come home to warmth and love but Agnes's eclipse of cheer was unyielding and allowed him no relief. He felt increasingly tired and ill. His teeth and gums had been troubling him recently although the dentist could not locate a specific problem. He had suggested extracting a couple of molars in the area where there was most discomfort but Willie wanted to hang on to his remaining teeth, so he had decided to wait a while and see if the pains settled. There was also a tender spot beneath his ribs and he was having trouble sleeping.

Most nights he tossed and turned till he wakened her. She would seethe with anger at his restlessness. He had long ago given up thoughts of physical comfort from her and she had made it clear that she was no longer to be bothered with such basic things now that the children were grown up and she was in middle age. Nevertheless, Willie liked bodily contact and settled for the scant comfort of cuddling her from behind, moulding his pliable body to her rigid sleeping shape. She seldom turned to face him now. He would read a lot when he could not sleep and sometimes he wrote verses, but only for himself.

It was on one such fraught night that he rose in the early hours to pace the floor in a vain attempt to find some relief. He lit the tilley and went to the bookcase where he thumbed through the leather bound volumes until he found the one that Agnes had given him for Christmas: the latest Conan Doyle, "The Hound of the Baskervilles." He liked Sherlock Holmes but he could not seem to concentrate on the plot so, after reading the same few pages over and over, he put it back on the shelf. He noticed that his clammy fingers had developed a slight involuntary tremor and were stained green from the dye in the leather cover.

He pulled a curtain. There was almost a full moon. The hills still held a smear of snow in patches which reflected brilliantly against the bare black rocky hillside. He pressed his brow against the glass, listening to the inevitable howl of the wind. Little flurries of white dust could be seen periodically gusting across the dark earth. The water in the voe rippled audibly and he saw traces of the aurora borealis in the northern sky. The wisps of astral iridescence had a hypnotic effect on him as they flitted like spectres across the vastness of the heavens. He wished his ailing mortal body could dissipate and blend with the dancers. Suddenly aware of a cold ache in his forehead, he stepped back . . . The raw night scene framed by the window was undeniably beautiful yet lonely and desolate. It matched his spirit.

The Westminster clock struck four and the chimes came loud and intruding, unnaturally prolonged. It was funny how things grew so out of proportion during the night, he thought. Small worries became magnified, time had no normal units. He was a troubled man, fearing for his health. He suspected that his symptoms might have a more sinister diagnosis than his light-hearted dismissal of them. The shortness of breath was getting worse. He touched the lump beneath the right lower margin of his rib cage, gasping as pain knotted his abdomen. Reluctantly, he accepted that he would have to seek a second opinion. He hoped that his anxiety would become insignificant in the proportional reality of morning. Perhaps it was the middle age crisis, whatever that was.

He was forty-five and until recently he had felt like a

twenty year old. He had worn fairly well with only one small bald patch in his reddish brown hair. He had a drooping dark moustache, peppered with grey, giving him a distinguished air. The lines of laughter around his eyes and the dimple on his chin gave him still a youthful appearance. He had always been relatively short in stature, although he felt secure in his 5ft 7ins. For a while during his teens, he had doubted that he would ever catch up with his contemporaries: "Willie erse-in-pockets" they had called him at school. His pubertal growth spurt had been late and he had been thankful for it. He was well built, not exactly muscular but firm and broad shouldered with narrow hips and well shaped legs, ever so slightly bowed, causing him to swagger when he walked. He was one of those lucky people who had an instant "presence." He was not unattractive though far from handsome. His chief attributes were his keen mind and warm personality.

He sat down again on his favourite chair. It was worn at the arms and he picked at the horsehair stuffing which was peeping through a hole in the faded wine coloured cloth. He held the strands to his nose, reflecting on the ponies he had cherished as a boy. He quickly threw the tufts into the kishie of peats on the hearth: they smelt of stale smoke and hair oil. Gone was the warm sweaty equine aroma. Gone like his youth.

He reached into the bag where he kept his stationery. He opened a notebook and wrote a short poem, straight from his heart, in his beloved dialect:

"A Glisk i da Winter Mirk.

> *When winds blew caald fae aff da haaf,*
> *An grey cloods on black deeps lay,*
> *A shrood spread ower a laand, sna-greemet, drear*
> *An ice strack dreed itae da hert*
> *As daeth stuid beckoning dere."*

No sooner had he composed the bleak lines than he scritted his pen through them and threw the pad into the bag. "Come awa noo," he told himself. " Du's no tae be sae doonhearted. Dat's no lik dee ava, boy. Dir's likely naethin wrang wi' dee but oweractive imagination."

He trooped back to bed. As he sought elusive sleep, he resolved to visit his colleague, in Lerwick.

———————

104

Sometimes it is quite possible to go for years without encountering a specific unusual object, or word, or person. Then again, the unexpected may occur several times in quick succession. So it was with Willie and Jean.

It was on Thursday evening that he arrived at Dr. Gordon MacKenzie's surgery. He had not told his friend that he was coming but simply hoped to catch him, quietly, after his evening session. The clinic was running late and two patients were still waiting on the bench. One of them was Jean. He was pleased to see her and they smiled and both said "Hello again!" and laughed at the clash of voices.

The other patient was Bella Beastie. Jean was wary of her, having heard the rumours, but her logic told her that the poor woman was no more than a frail old lady who sucked peppermints with loud slurping noises and drummed idle fingers on the wooden arms of her chair. Jean smiled, wondering why people thought her an evil omen. The witchy wife stared at Jean with vacant eyes and did not return the greeting. She was dressed in black and had wispy grey hair escaping from a headscarf and random clumps of whiskers stemming from an abundance of moles on a wrinkled face. She was stiff and slow on her feet when she was called. As she shuffled past, she stopped. As Jean looked at her, wondering why she hesitated, she was filled with a feeling of unease, almost panic. It quickly passed as the old woman moved on. Bella Beastie's consultation turned out to be a long one allowing Jean and Willie time to cement their acquaintance.

Fate works in mysterious ways and human attraction has no rules. Sometimes one meets a stranger and the chemistry is right for an instant and lasting friendship. So it was with them. It is difficult to explain. It could be argued that Jean lacked a depth of discourse in her life, true communication with an allied spirit. For Willie's part, he was uncharacteristically depressed and this woman's exuberance reached out to him so that his heart and mind embraced human interest again with the realisation that he was not alone in what currently seemed like a great vast void. The stark contrast between Jean and his wife was part of the attraction.

Jean told him that she had come for belated confirmation of her pregnancy. Willie, less forthright, played down his own worst fears and said that he had routine medical matters to discuss with his colleague.

She enquired about Billy. He said there was no fresh news, only that Agnes had written and wanted him home as soon as possible. They talked easily and freely about many things, including their mutual love of music and poetry.

"Dr. Leask, do you ken that ye're easy to speak till . . . I've always had difficulty relating t' Shetland folk, to tell the truth."

"I'm no surprised, Jean", he said with a chuckle. "We hae a tendency to spaek in cryptic messages. Although we understand each idder weel enough, ootsiders . . . if you'll pardon the expression . . . they're usually a bit confused by wir communication system."

When she was called, she was sorry to leave his company and knew that the feeling was mutual. They both also knew that their friendship would be impossible to sustain. They lived in different places, had diverging lifestyles. They would seldom meet fortuitously.

"Where does du bide, Jean?" he ventured to ask as she rose. "I hae an excellent peerie book on the management of pregnancy. I would be happy to lend it tae dee if du'd care to hiv it."

"Oh . . . aye, 'at would be most helpful, Dr. Leask. Eh...it would be best if you dropped it in at Robertson's during a weekday. I work from 8.30 till 5.30 . . . I get a break at one o'clock."

"Right den, A'll dae dat. I'm often i' da toon for one reason or anidder. Hit's nae trouble . . . Goodbye, Jean."

On the following Tuesday, he brought the book. It was approaching one when he came and she was able to knock off a few minutes early. It was a fine bright April day. Willie had made sure that he had an hour to spare and it seemed entirely natural for them to walk and talk and enjoy each other's company. They wandered through the south end, past the Lodberries and up round the Knab. The sunshine was warm and wispy clouds cast dappled shadows over the green grass and the cliffs. Fulmars were already claiming nest sites on the ledges and the clear shrill song of a laverick played high overhead. Spring was in the air and there was a spring in Willie's step. They spoke of local news: the continuing recession in the fishing industry; the flu epidemic; whether Lerwick was still a safe place for children in view of the recent reports.

Jean confided the rumours concerning Gideon and the

scathing comments she'd overheard about her own brother. His introverted behaviour was certainly a source of worry, she said, although she could detect no malice in him. Willie explained to her that many teenagers went through a personality turmoil.

"... so, dinna du be influenced by idle gossip. Help him to get ower his troubles. Gie him support, Jean. Dinna alienate him. Dinna drive him awa lik we did wir Billy. Your bridder will share many characteristics wi' yoursel . . . so I canna tink he is a bad egg."

She listened to the advice. He was so homely, sincere, yet she could not forget the strange incident so long ago.

"Do you believe in prophetic dreams, Dr. Leask?"

"Du should caa me Willie, Jean. Yes, I do. I believe that strange messages fae da past and da future can come to wis. I also think dat some fok are much mair susceptible tae dis than idders."

"Have you ever experienced any yourself?"

"No, nothing lik dat. I do sense things sometimes . . ." he looked at her and hesitated ". . . but hit's usually to do wi' me work and probably just reflects me training. My faider noo, he had strong psychical senses. I mind him telling a story o' when he was just a boy o' nineteen and he was invited tae a caerdin . . . Does du ken what dat is?"

"No."

"Weel, a caerdin is a traditional Shetland gadderin o' young lasses, usually in da country places. Dey meet tae caerd and spin the wool after clipping time. It is a great social occasion, and there is often a bit of a foy. Da young men geen alang sometimes to court." He smiled, his eyes twinkling with mischief.

"Aye."

"Weel, my faider was wance on his wye to one in the early evening when he saw a light shining fae below a peerie brig. He went to da source but couldna fin ony trace o' it. He was intrigued but no particularly worried because dying sunlight on water can play strange tricks on da human eye. It had been a fine hairst day and his shadow was cast in front o' him.

Weel, after dat odd incident, he had dis strong sensation dat he should turn back. Den he saw a second shadow moving alongside his ain. There was naebody else there and the feeling dat he must go back grew so strong dat he became a bit scared. By dis time, though, he was nearing his

107

destination and hit was a lang journey back. Also, he had his eye on a young lass dat wid be dere. Weel, he pressed on, greatly relieved when he entered da hoose and da shadow left him.

He had an enjoyable night. Hooever, one o' da girls present was incubating a case o' measles . . . she was at the infectious stage, before the rash appears. My faider contracted the disease a fortnight later and passed it on tae his younger bridder, wha wisna a strong bairn. He died."

The story was eerie. It was also impressive. It fed her imagination. Willie continued:

"So, despite such omens, I think we'll always follow wir ain instincts, whatever. I believe in being true to my fellow man and woman and.."

"Div ye believe in God, Willie?"

"Yes, I have faith in a force greater than mere mortals although I do sometimes hiv me doubts. This bloody war and the aftermath of illness and suffering . . . hit's difficult to accept that yun's God's will! I think I'd be kinda faert no tae believe that there's something bigger and better. I certainly thanked the Lord when I learned wir Billy was alive."

The hour passed quickly. Their relationship was endorsed.

"I'll look in again, Jean, if du widna mind? Tak dee time wi' da book." He waved goodbye a few yards from her workplace.

———

That evening, long after Agnes had gone to bed, he sat in his chair and fiddled with the horsehair padding. It had been confirmed that he had a growth in his chest. It was likely that his right lung was affected by cancer. He would have to go to Aberdeen for further X-rays and tests to establish whether his liver was healthy and to determine his prognosis. He knew that he was terminally ill yet the knowledge had somehow reduced his fear. He could face it now.

He pondered on recent events, thinking of Jean who seemed to fill his mind every waking moment although he barely knew her and did not understand why she touched his heart so easily . . . nor did he need to comprehend. It was enough that she did. He had no serious notion of a romantic liaison. He knew they were both married people and that she was young, her life ahead of her. Nevertheless, he yearned for her.

He pulled out his writing pad again and resurrected his abandoned verse. This time the finished article had a note of optimism:

> When winds blew caald fae aff da haaf,
> An grey cloods on black deeps lay,
> A shrood spread ower a laand, sna-greemet, drear
> An ice strack dreed itae da hert
> As daeth stuid beckoning dere.
>
> But dan du cam, wi dee laachin een,
> Glansin, sunsheen dancin on da waves,
> An brocht back hopp ageen
> O warmth an life renewed
> An memories o love lang geen.
>
> In dremms Ah'll see dee still,
> A peerie glint fae heeven's shore
> At fills me hert wi happiness
> Troo aa da darkness yet in store
> Till faer an caald an winter er no more.
>
> So come du back wi dee boanny smile,
> Come du back lik da mayflooer i da voar,
> An bide du dan, bide a langer while,
> Till riggs lie green an life sings oot wi joy
> An nychts growe closser, waarmer, saft,
> Wi winds but whispered promises made new."

He laid the notebook aside and went to his bed. Agnes seemed to be asleep, her face to the wall. He cuddled up and touched her shoulder. She stiffened and shrugged his hand away. His heart ached.

17

Church Bells and Alarm Bells

The ration books were abolished on 3rd May 1919. However, money was scarce, especially in the fishermen's pockets since overseas herring markets were depressed, with both Russia and Germany, the prospective giant consumers, inaccessible to business. James West constantly struggled to make ends meet and to avoid falling deeper into debt, but like the rest of the fishermen, he was much relieved when the Fishmarket resumed sales on 3 June, after a five year shut-down. However, much of the catch still went to the kippering kilns and prices remained abysmally low. Consequently, large quantities of herring were dumped or sold to the gutfactory for the manufacture of manure.

There were fairly good landings of whiting and large flat-fish but, ironically, there was no reliable commercial market for these species. In the first week of June, the Burra boat "Exceed" did exceed the halibut record by landing a 306lb giant, over 7 ft in length and 3 ft. across the fins. Many specimens approaching the same size were landed in Lerwick and, in common with many Scottie families, Jean and James dined frequently on halibut.

In desperation, a meeting of fishermen was called in early summer. By combining forces against the opportunistic buyers, they agreed to stick rigidly to a minimum price of £2 per cran for herring. There was a rare feeling of unity among them, Scotties and Shetlanders alike. Port strikes were called at Fraserburgh and Peterhead in similar protest over poor prices. In the wake of war and in the face of financial adversity, racial segregation in the town lessened and mixed crews were soon operating on a few local boats.

This spirit of unity was further consolidated by the Peace Day celebrations on Saturday, 19 July. It was grey, overcast weather but a buoyant mood persisted among the revellers who lined the streets. A fluttering forest of flags and banners brightened up Commercial Street, the Hillhead, Market Street and Burgh Road. These were draped from gates, windows, washing lines and even from the few arthritic tree limbs that cowered behind gale-proof garden walls and grew horizontally once they became exposed to the relentless elements of these northern climes. The fishing boats at Alexandra Wharf displayed bunting and the brass band marched from the Poorhouse to the Town Hall and meandered through the main streets ending up in the North Road.

Jean was six months pregnant and small for her dates although otherwise in good health following her earlier bouts of nausea. Infected by the merriment, she joined the procession of marchers with Mary, Elsie, her brothers and sister, and James. It was a joyful day although, beneath the flamboyant froth of celebration, people were filled with a deep-rooted sadness for their lost loved ones.

Many of the local merchants and businessmen had organised a works country outing for the afternoon. Jean's employers were no exception and the J.W. Robertson's trip was to Whiteness. She had never been there before, although she knew the West side as far as Tingwall and Gott and was well acquainted with the South mainland via the sea rather than the land. She had often sailed with her father as far as the island of Mousa. Usually by then she was seasick, so she would be transferred aboard a passing harbour-bound boat.

She was excited, particularly since she had heard so much about Whiteness from Willie. He had actually popped in to see her several times and been introduced to James on one occasion. James liked him instantly and saw no threat in his pregnant wife keeping company with this older man: he seemed to do her good and did not charge for his sensible professional advice about diet and exercise either. He also lent her helpful books. Jean suspected that Willie was unwell and she was not surprised that he had not been in to see her for a fortnight because he had said that he was due to visit Aberdeen shortly on medical business.

James was invited to the outing. However, on the same day, he was also required to attend an official R.N.M.D.S.F. function. Jean, however, resolved to go along with her workmates and share in the festivities. Soon her advancing pregnancy would impinge on her ability to work full hours. Yet she needed to keep earning as long as possible. Perhaps she'd be able to take advantage of the general goodwill of the occasion and might negotiate a part time opportunity.

A small convoy of hooded horse carriages had been hired.

Jean sat beside Edith, the wife of a colleague, as they set off on the adventure.

Edith was a mousy character, lacking self-confidence and anxious to please. She had been about forty years old for a decade and presented an ageless ample figure. Her beady eyes watered a lot and her thin pouting lips sported a faint moustache. She sometimes reminded Jean of a shrew with the sulks but she was really a shy and pleasant person and Jean was glad of her undemanding company. Edith meant well. She was always willing to help and yet, in practical terms, was usually more of a hindrance.

The horses kept up a good pace over the dozen or so miles to Whiteness, slowing down where the road was rutted and the carriage springs made warning groans, then trotting on again when the temporary obstacle course was clear. The surface was rough at best and puddle pocked in the worst stretches. Sheep grazed everywhere and twice the driver had to slow down as a semi-weaned lamb tempted fate and fled to its mother grazing on the opposite side. Probably sheep in Shetland outnumbered people, Jean mused.

Her mood changed to an overwhelming appreciation of the view from the top of Wormadale. The coastline could be traced all the way to the southerly tip of the mainland, where Fitful Head was swathed in a mantle of mist. The sea was alive with bright patches as numerous vertical shafts of sunlight pierced through grey cloud and fell on calm waters. A variety of little islands lay to the South and West, dark shapes against the horizon as far as the eye could see. The inbye islets, the holms, seemed almost touchable. She minded Billy Leask: "I'll sha dee da holms in Whiteness one day, Jean, if du liks?" She smiled and pressed her cheek against the cold carriage window, making moist breath marks on the glass, then wiping them off with her sleeve.

Arriving at their destination, the trippers bustled out of their seats and the peace of rural Whiteness was shattered by happy sounds: clatter and singing, cheering and laughter. Glad to be pulled up, a sweating horse relieved itself, the large brown steaming dollops slapping down on to the metalled road. Several others emulated this action and there was a chorus of horses breaking wind, like a series of protracted punctures. Jean harmonised with a long laughing sigh and followed Edith into a field. Tents had been pitched the previous day and these were soon complemented by folding tables and chairs. There was food aplenty and there were games, tugs-of-war and races. The children were ecstatic and the adults became children. Peace Day was celebrated to the full. Jean avoided athletic games although she helped to keep scores. She indulged herself with a glass of cider.

Around three o'clock she felt dizzy and decided the drink had gone to her head. Edith fussed and suggested a stroll. There was a well-used bye-road into South Whiteness and they wandered in that direction, past a small church and several crofts. After a mile or so, beside some Standing Stones, they stopped to hail a hardy old woman. She responded with a wave and a nod, being preoccupied with shifting a ram on a tether. The horned creature was stubborn but the crofter's will was stronger. She muttered at the tup in broad dialect, an incomprehensible garble of sounds to the Lerook visitors although they inferred the gist of the meaning.

They laughed and followed the track. A smell of peat smoke permeated the air by a ramshackle dwelling which looked uninhabited. It was in an advanced state of disrepair and was surrounded by parallelogram sheds and outhouses. However, smoke rose from the chimney. A man and a youth were busy earthing up potatoes. They were both lean and arachnid, the adult pock-marked and the adolescent with pubertal pimples. They seemed wary of the strangers, tentatively lifting their hoes in greeting but offering no words.

It had begun to drizzle as they turned back and the blackening skies heralded a heavy downpour. That was when the first pains came, making her double up and cry out. She sat on a rock in an attempt to ease the agony, while her flustered companion minced and fluttered on the grassy bank, unable to offer any coherent course of action. Luckily they were quite close to the old woman's cottage. Edith was a neurotic wreck by the time they eventually struggled into Willa Leask's porch. She had lost her hat but did not seem to notice.

"Feth, what ails you, lasses?" Willa said, "Come awa in and set her apo da restin chair, get her feet up noo."

Willa took charge. She gave Edith snappy instructions about how to reach the doctor's house, three miles away. She said it was lucky that the doctor, her nephew, was staying in Whiteness this week. She asked Jean a lot of questions.

"Du'd better tell wir Willie tae bring his machine and some o' yun chlariform," she told Edith.

She insisted that Jean should drink a cup of hot sweet tea, which made her feel a little better although she was in a panic, aware that it was much too early and something must be wrong. Willa, however, was a comfort. She said that she had helped deliver many a premature bairn. Willie would arrive shortly, she reassured, "if yun fat freend o' dine kin run fast enough in her silly toon shön." Then she disappeared to get ". . . twartree things at we'll need." She returned brandishing a cut-throat razor.

Jean stared. "Fit are ye gaain to do wi' 'at?" she managed to say.

"Feth, hit's tae keep da trows awa fae da bairn," Willa replied, surprised that Jean did not know of this essential ritual. She proceeded to place the blade and a silver threepenny piece under the cushion of the wooden resting chair upon which Jean was reclining. Then she placed a tattered copy of the Holy Book and an enamel basin full of dirty washing-up water on the table beside Jean's head. Jean looked suspiciously at the filthy liquid with bits of oily debris floating in it. Willa smiled.

"Niver huve oot dirty water till da clean be in," she muttered on her way out the door with a pail to fetch a fresh supply from the well.

The pains subsided. When Willie arrived, Jean was smiling and most apologetic about causing alarm. Nevertheless, he insisted on checking.

There was no evidence of malady in pulse or blood pressure, he informed her, and the baby still had vital movement and a faint echo of a heartbeat. However, her temperature was high and there had been some bleeding. He was gentle and competent. She felt completely at ease with him, friend and physician. He explained that false alarms were fairly frequent in pregnancy and suggested that this one had been induced by overactivity. She would have to take it easier from now on and do nothing strenuous to provoke nature.

Despite her protests, he insisted on driving her home. He made her promise to take things at an invalid pace over the weekend and not to hesitate to call Dr. MacKenzie on Monday, or earlier if necessary. "Should it start again, you must contact him straight away," he emphasised.

James thanked him for his concern and the two men

shared a rare glass of whisky. It was a peaceful end to Peace Day.

———

She felt fine on Sunday morning and there was not a trace of the previous day's symptoms. Perhaps it had been indigestion, or the cider. She was determined not to miss their weekly attendance at the church service. After all, it was to be a special commemorative meeting and there would be nothing strenuous about walking the short distance and sitting in a pew.

Lerwick Parish Church was filled to capacity and there was standing room only when they arrived. In addition to representatives from the Town Council, there were officials from Zetland County Council and Admiral Greatorex (C.B. M.V.O.) and his staff. Clergymen from all the local churches also attended this unique gathering: Rev. E. W. Greensheild, R.N.M.D.S.F. (A friend of James, from the Mission); ministers from St. Olaf's and St. Ringan's United Free churches; clergy from the Baptist Church and from St. Magnus Episcopal.

She was glad not to have missed the event and wondered why she had ever doubted her faith in recent years. There was a riveting address by Dr. Wilcock of St. Ringans and passages were read from the old testament book of Isaiah. The church choir sang a lovely version of "To Thee, O Lord, We Fly" and the mass voices of the congregation blended powerfully to sing "Praise My Soul, the King of Heaven."

As the lengthy sermon progressed, she felt the weight of the baby pressing heavily on her bladder and pelvic floor. Her back ached with the standing and she tried to concentrate on the words:

"... the question as to the relationship between Christianity and war was one that troubled many during the time of strife...if the offender strikes me on one cheek, I am to turn to him the other ... 'Dear Lord, don't let me faint or disgrace myself in this church', she prayed ... so far as Christianity is opposed to Warfare, it is itself a warfare, Michael and his Angels warring against the devil and his angels ..."

She felt another war raging within herself. She sensed too that it would be a long painful time until it was won... or lost. She longed for a seat and relief from the pressing leaden weight of the womb. She shuffled, not wanting to draw attention to herself. She tightened her urinary sphincter muscles and gritted her teeth. Surely she was not going to wet herself in church, God forbid. She silently thanked the Lord when the sermon ended. She leaned heavily on James's arm, pale and drawn.

They filed out slowly, dropping a florin into the box. The collection was earmarked for the Princess Louise's Scottish Hospital for limbless sailors and soldiers.

They stopped several times to rest. She relieved herself in a stranger's backyard privy near the kirk, worrying all the while that she was trespassing on somebody else's property. James stood guard, ready to explain the emergency but the place remained deserted. At home, she went straight to bed. She was unwell but felt no labour pains as such. James heated a large rounded beach stone in the oven and wrapped it in an old seaboot sock to stop it from burning the bedclothes. She lay on her side and held the welcome warmth to her abdomen. The baby kicked strongly in response. She closed her eyes and, between waves of nausea, faces flashed before her . . . Willie . . . Bella Beastie. She spoke silently to the unborn extension of herself: I fear all is not well with thee, my little one, but I will try my best.

18

Hidden Yearning

That evening, James summoned Elsie for a few days. Elsie, he reasoned, would be more sensible than Mary should a crisis develop. There was not a dottled hair in the old lady's head and she and Jean got on well together. He could not afford to stay home from the fishing and, anyway, Jean insisted she was fine: it was the prolonged standing that had made her unwell. Still, the pains in her lower abdomen and back niggled on. Dr. MacKenzie was sent for and he ordered complete rest or else miscarriage was likely. Jean reluctantly agreed to stay in bed.

Monday was one of those peculiar days when visitors appeared from everywhere, partly because Elsie had spread the word that Jean was poorly. Edith came, bringing fruit and fussing. Young Helen Hepburn, a good friend and neighbour brought her two little girls and a newly made batch of oatcakes. The Hepburns were a happy family although they were not well off. Helen's husband, Tom, was almost stone deaf after a war explosion. Consequently, he had experienced difficulty getting employment and took casual work whenever he could. The jobs never lasted long: there had been several incidents where his impaired hearing had almost caused an accident. Unemployment was high, especially among the coopers. A good stock of barrels had been built up, but demand for them remained low, and now the two largest Lerwick cooperages were standing practically idle. Still, Tom was determined to provide for Helen and his two daughters, Christina and Ruth. James had taken him aboard as a deck-hand now and then, assigning him limited tasks. Johnie had recently helped him establish a fish round in the town. This suited him better and Helen gutted and filleted the fish.

Helen was a beautiful woman who worked hard and had little time for frivolity. The girls had both inherited their mother's good looks and their father's stubborness and humour. Tom loved to play with his lasses and they teased him constantly, taking full advantage of his deafness. They hid when he came home, and pounced, knowing that he would pretend to rage and chase them. Ruth, four years old, had never mastered the difficult art of sleeping all night without wetting the bed. Her mother grumbled but Tom dismissed it as a normal phase of growing up. He made a joke of all such things and the children thrived on his humour and were secure and trusting in their environment.

Thus, when Willie arrived, Jean's house was full of women. He accepted their invitation to share a plate of broth and oatcakes. He laughed and joked with them and charmed the children. Ruth, in particular, took a great liking to him. She was an endearing child. She sat at his feet and rummaged in his open bag, bringing forth his notebook. He retrieved the open pad, saying:

"Yun's no very interesting, Ruth, hit's just twartree scraps o' poetry dat I write for me ain amusement. Let's pit it awa, will we?"

"I ken a poem too," said the youngster.

"Does du, noo . . . Weel, let's hear it then?"

"A rift is just a gust of wind . . ."

She was cut short by her mother: "Ruthie! . . . 'At's nae fit t'repeat in company." Turning to the others, she said: "'At's her faither's bad influence. He's an affa man, teaching the quines 'at rubbish."

"Oh, let her go on wi' it," Willie encouraged, "I lik ony kind o' poetry. I'd lik tae hear Ruth's rhyme."

The child looked to her frowning mother, then at the smiling stranger. Christina sniggered. Ruth took a step towards him and continued in a low voice that gathered volume as she revelled in the performance:

> *"A rift is just a gust of wind,*
> *Proceeding from the heart,*
> *But when it takes the downward course,*
> *It's often called a fart.*

Christina sniggered.

> *A fart's a very useful thing,*
> *It gives the body ease.*
> *It warms the bed on a winter's night*
> *And it scares away the fleas."*

Everybody laughed. Willie patted her on the head and

nodded his approval. A blushing Helen Hepburn said it was time to leave and ushered the girls out the door.

"Willie, I ken ye'll no accept onything," Jean said when they were alone, ". . . and I hiv nithing tae gie . . . but here are some lucky keepsakes for you. They are worth nithing yet I like to collect the pretty ones." She handed him three spherical pearls, perfect examples of their kind, the pride and glory of many years of splitting mussels.

He peered at the creamy glistening peerie beauties in his palm and felt pleasure:

"Dir's nae need tae thank me, Jean. Du's as welcome as da mayflooers i' da voar . . . But I shall treasure them always, as if they sprang fae da Queen o' da Sea hersel."

His own troubles and yearnings remained hidden, the confused thoughts reflected only in verses, penned for himself alone. Poetry helped to express his complicated feelings. He understood himself better then, the nebulous wandering thoughts becoming precise and tangible through the liberating power of familiar dialect. He wrote with simple unadulterated honesty. A poem appeared in his notebook in the early hours of Tuesday, 22 July:

> "Du shone dere among dem aa;
> Me eyes saa only dee.
> Whan du cam near, me hert sang,
> Wi da love du brocht ta me.
> Du is nae fancy toy, nae passin ploy,
> Du is me lovely lass, life's first and hidmost joy.
>
> But years divide wi idder ties,
> So du haes dine an I hae mine,
> Wir gaets geen idder wyes.
> O dat I'd funn dee lang fae syne,
> Whin time and flesh could melt and mell
> Dee an me in life-renewing bliss."

He had been to Aberdeen. His cancer was confirmed. There was little to be done and he knew that his life expectancy was twelve to eighteen months at best. He resolved to make his peace with people, especially Agnes. Most of the time he displayed great strength and courage but, occasionally, an inner terror of enormous magnitude took over his being. Only thinking of Jean helped him through these panic attacks. He reached into his waistcoat pocket and fondled the comforting little pearls. They soothed him, like worry beads, bestowing a certain measure of peace.

He longed to see Billy again. He would make a journey South, he determined, if his son was not discharged in the next few months.

———————

Jean spent a restless night, tossing and turning, eyelids fluttering, sweat glistening on her forehead. She thrashed and twisted, clutching spasmodically at the bedclothes and falling in and out of a patchy dream:

She floated out of her bed. It was strange to be hovering, weightless, high above the ground, her arms and legs propelling her through the night air. She could feel the embossed paper on the kitchen walls with her fingertips as she reached downwards towards the door handle. She swam breast-stroke along the twilit street, aware of a yellow red glow from the midnight sun as it skirted the sky from east to west, barely dipping below the horizon. She was heading towards the harbour

It was so effortless to swim along the Burgh Road, glancing into the sleeping houses through high windows. She had to gasp for breath, though, as the air seemed thinner. It was cold.

She was worried. She must hurry to the West Dock. She wore only flimsy night attire. She stopped to tug the night-gown over her pregnant belly and backside. She dreaded meeting anyone but there was no living soul around. She floated in silent loneliness.

She felt an evil force. Something invisible stalked the ground below. Then . . . there was salt water in her nostrils, stinging her throat. She held her breath . . . gasped for air . . . she was choking . . . an icy claw snatched at her legs . . .

Her heart pounded with terror . . . There was a soft knocking at the door . . .

CHAPTER
19
'Tis an ill Wind

"Hold on a minute. I'm coming," she called. She was swollen and cumbersome and had to rock a couple of times to gain the momentum to raise herself from the mattress. As she got her feet to the floor, the outside door creaked open and somebody came in. She heard soft footsteps on the scullery waxcloth.

"Is 'at you, Johnie? . . . James? . . ." She waddled through but there was nobody there. It was quite empty. There was nowhere to hide. She shivered. The words of her grandmother came into her mind: "Somebody coming in, Jean, means somebody going oot. Dinna bar the door to the knock."

She tried the handle. It was unlocked as usual. She lit the lamp and sidled from one room to the other, trying to sense her visitor, the air heavy with expectancy. There was nothing, no one.

She made tea. There would be no more sleep this night.

A wan faced Johnie brought the news the following morning. He did not have to speak. One look at his haggard features and she knew. The strong sense of foreboding, the knocking and the visitation, were neither fantasy nor dream. James was gone. She held Johnie's slim troubled form tightly and together they cried.

Later she learned the detail. It was a freak accident. As the net was shot, James was caught in the ropes and dragged overboard. There was a thick fog and he had been pulled under by the weight of the gear. By the time the crew recovered his body, it was too late. Johnie had frantically tried to resuscitate him, refusing to accept the inevitable. They said that he was like a creature possessed, with superhuman strength. It had taken three men to drag him off the corpse and slap him into reality. He had been very quiet ever since.

He stayed with Jean during the following days and she was glad. The windows were black blinded as her husband's body was laid out in the front room. Many mourners came and paid their respects. Superintendent John Shewan from the Mission came with deepest sympathy and practical help in the form of a box of groceries. Gideon Pouffe came to pray with her, to bring her the comfort of the Almighty and the great Book. Unlike Gideon, however, she could not find her oblivion in the scriptures. She felt disgusted by him, his pretentious claptrap, his whole personality . . . perhaps there was something in the rumours. Her younger brothers and sisters came too, nervous and sober faced, too young to understand the rituals of death. They were not at school due to the summer holidays being officially extended by one week throughout the entire country in commemoration of the Peace.

There is no peace, thought Jean. She sat quietly in a corner and maintained a dry-eyed vigil for two days. She could not face her own mother or James's mother. Johnie took over and made many cups of tea. With a curious dignity that needed no words to convey it, he took charge of the wake. Money was scarce. There was the doctor's bill of £6 2s 6d for certifying the death. Then there were the burial costs and Jean wanted a decent headstone.

Unaware that James had ever approached Silas Smith, Johnie made his way to the moneylender's premises. He recognised the young man at the counter. He had seen him hanging around the docks in the early morning, a bit of a loner like himself. The sallow faced assistant began to explain that his father dealt with only regular customers, when Silas himself appeared.

"That's correct, Mr . . . eh . . . I have only established clients as a rule." The collar-and-tie youth scuttled away into the back shop. He seemed nervous.

"Weel, the circumstances are afa urgent . . ." Johnie began. He was cut short as soon as his doric accent betrayed his origins:

"I don't care to hear about it, boy. I don't wish to deal with Scotties . . . You're not welcome here. There are too many strangers in this town. It's not a safe place to live anymore . . . full of queer characters . . . like that perverted preacher . . . and God knows what else!"

It was futile to persist against such bias. Johnie gazed at the man and shook his head. Jean would have to wait for a headstone. He would find some way of paying the other expenses.

The days following the funeral passed in a blur for Jean: she remained silent and troubled while Johnie continued to organise matters. Their roles were reversed: she became introverted and the extreme crisis of the situation was strangely therapeutic for him. He was needed.

Expressions of sympathy arrived from friends and neighbours. Willie sent a short note:

"Dearest Jean,
I send heart-felt sympathy. I have no adequate words. Please do not hesitate to seek my help if there is anything you need.
Your friend,
Willie."

She wondered why he did not come in person and yet she was relieved that he did not. There was an intensity about him that she could not admit at this time. There was nothing that anyone could do. James was buried on 8th August. They had been married seven months.

CHAPTER

20

Troubled Waters

Jean insisted that Johnie move out after the funeral. She wanted some quiet time for herself and promised she would take things slowly and not be overactive. After all, she reasoned, she must get used to her own company again and the baby was not due for two months. She did not want to go back home; there was no room and, anyway, she had come to value her privacy. Willie came to see her on 9th August and she felt the better of his visit. She knew he would come again.

It was during the night of 10th August that her waters burst. She had suffered backache all day and had just sunk exhausted into the healing crypt of sleep when she was jolted again into unwelcome consciousness. She was alone in the house.

This was no false alarm: several pints of amniotic fluid soaked the bedclothes and the dull ache gave way quickly to gripping labour pains, fast and furious palpitations, making her cry out. She tried to time them, but there seemed to be no persistent pattern. She could not concentrate. She shouted for help, but Flora West, whose bedroom was closest, was very deaf. The old man slept in the room at the back and did not hear her.

She rose from the bed in a brief lull between the spasms that knotted her abdomen and hurt her entire body. She knocked a shoe on the wall. Nobody heard her. As the contractions strengthened and walloped her again and again, she tried to get ease by lying on her back, her side, her knees. She called for her mother, Elsie, James . . . Willie. She dropped to her knees on the rag rug and said in a panting whisper:

"Help me, dear Lord."

There was no relief. She squirmed around the floor, curling into the foetal position when the worst pains came and skirling without shame for her nearest and dearest, knowing all the while that there was nobody. She had no idea how long she writhed in painful labour, but the sun was well up in the sky and she was soaking and totally exhausted. Still no baby came. She was sure it was no longer alive, that no little creature could survive such trauma. She felt now she could endure it no longer. She did not care if she lived or died. It was then that Johnie came.

He lost no time. He summoned the doctor and Elsie. In the interim, he busied himself without a blush, changing the wet linen and lifting his sister from floor to bed. She was grey and darkened strands of clammy hair stuck to her forehead. She looked terrible. She reminded him of a drowned face.

Elsie was the first to arrive and the baby was stillborn shortly before the doctor came at nine-fifteen in the morning of 11th August. Without a word, Elsie wrapped the tiny bloodstained body in a clean pillowslip and went to take it to the other room.

"Gie me m' child." Jean whimpered, her tears welling and a different ache permeating her being.

"Best nae to look upon her, Jeanie, m'quine."

"I have to hold her, Grandma."

The infant was a pinkish purple colour, not much bigger than a six week old kitten. Jean saw only beauty. The miniature features seemed perfect to her as she felt for the tiny hand and stroked the damp head with its sprinkling of hair. The eyes were closed, never having seen the light of day. The curved blue-tinged lips had not parted to inhale a single breath. There was a harelip. She barely noticed it. She clung to the luke-warm infant and wept for her child, for James . . . and for herself. The pain in her heart was all absorbing and she was completely submissive to its power. There was hopelessness. There was no anger.

The child was not right. It had several physical abnormalities. Elsie noticed right away that there were extra toes and fingers, the ears were set low, the eyes too close together. Jean did not seem to see these things and Elsie was relieved.

The doctor made a routine medical check, ensuring that the afterbirth had been expelled. He prescribed a mild sedative. He turned his attention to a brief examination of the stillbirth and entered the following report in his medical records:-

"WEST. Child born with multiple congenital anomalies including cleft lip and palate, hypotelorism and mid face

abnormalities, polydactyly of the hands and feet (a sixth finger on the left hand and an extra toe on each foot, set at an odd angle to the other five). There is a single umbilical artery. This may be a recognised syndrome of some sort, but a rare one."

He had not seen this particular spectrum of faults before. He asked permission to take the corpse away for a full examination. Elsie was glad to see the back of it.

He left two sleeping pills and said that he would call again later. Looking round the clean but sparsely furnished accommodation, he was aware that this family had poverty as well as tragedy to contend with and he offered to visit next day without additional charge. He asked whether Jean and her husband had been blood relatives and Elsie explained that James' mother was a Watt, a first cousin to Jean's father. Finding this explanation a little confusing, he later wrote in his notes,

"Some degree of consanguinity appears to be likely, but the parents are not as close as first cousins."

Nevertheless, the foetus had best be sent to Aberdeen for proper examination. He would leave it to the experts. Besides, if there was any hereditary reason for the abnormalities, it was perhaps unlikely that they would recur in any subsequent pregnancy since the poor woman's husband was dead.

The following days passed indistinctly for Jean, time and events were obscure and confused. Looking back years later, she had little memory of them. To her family and friends, she was seen to sit in a chair in the corner of the unlit room and rock backwards and forwards, her arms wrapped around her body, nursing the empty space where the baby had been and chewing on a strand of her own hair. She was chilled and empty. She wandered around the room, not seeing, not caring. The grand sight of a flotilla of fourteen American vessels in the harbour, one that thrilled the whole town, made her feel sick. What was there to celebrate?

Elsie came to stay and Willie to visit. Although she did speak to them about trivial matters, she seemed far away most of the time. He explained to Elsie that she had a shock-induced detachment from reality and that it was only a temporary condition. She was physically and mentally stable.

He thought to himself as he heard his own words that this was an inadequate phrase for interminable waiting . . . and he had so little time to give her.

CHAPTER
21
Caught

Helen Hepburn stepped out of the back door into the yard. She had been baking, hampered and aided by her youngest, Ruth, who had now lost interest in the odd shaped lumps of dough, streaked an unappetising dirty grey by tiny fingers. Helen shouted in a shrill voice towards the neighbouring garden where she could hear squabbling:

"Christina!...Where the divil are you, quine?"

Two heads appeared around the corner of the dyke, the younger with tears streaming.

" 'Ere ye'are . . . at it again, as soon as my back is turned! Chrissie, stop fighting with your sister and go and fetch me a message." She wiped her floury hands on her apron and pulled a sixpence from a pocket. "Here, get me a half pun' o' bilin' beef and a marrow bone fae the butcher in ower. Noo, dinna lose m'change . . . and fur goodness sake tak' Ruthie wi' ye oot o' my hair fur a whilie . . . You can ging the tap wye, up ower the Hillheed, there's a bittie less traffic though the lanes."

Chrissie frowned at her mother. She took the money and turned to yank Ruthie's hand in an exaggerated movement of reluctant obedience. It wasn't fair. She wanted to play with her own friends . . . not to have to trail this whining four-year-old all the way to Commercial Street. Still, she dare not refuse.

Ruthie tripped along behind complaining that the pace was too fast and clutching constantly at her sister's sleeve for towing anchorage. They went up the hill past the Town Hall and the wailing got louder as her legs grew tired. Turning into the top of Steep Close (now Hangcliff Lane), Chrissie said: "Look, A'm right scunnered wi' yer greeting! . . . you sit doon here till A rin doon an' get mam's message. A'll just be twa minutes. Aa right?"

The toddler was relieved to get a rest. She sat obediently on the stone step, immediately occupying herself by picking up a slater and rolling the squirming multilegged insect over onto its back. Christina ran down the hill.

Five minutes seemed like an eternity to Ruthie. Then he came up the lane, smiling.

"Hello, little girl . . . what are you doing?"

"Waiting fur m' sister."

He stared down at her, excitement bubbling through his veins. His voice was low and secretive when he spoke again: "I've got a bunny rabbit in a hutch," he said, pointing to a nearby yard, " Would you like to see it?"

"Ooo . . . aye . . . please."

Tiredness forgotten, the innocent followed Mr Hyde.

There was indeed a caged rabbit. It had an injured foot, near severed by a wire snare. Ruthie pressed her face to the hutch and peered at the fluffy creature. He knelt beside her. An involuntary tremor made his right eyelid twitch." He's hurt, mister . . . Look, he's bleeding." She proceeded to open the lid of the jagged box and then lifted the animal out. She felt its heart beating fast in its chest and its pink nose moved in rapid sympathy. She was unaware of a different rhythmic pulse that was gaining momentum in her companion. The fluffy captive seized its chance to flee, suddenly bolting out of her gentle grasp, leaving blood on her dress.

"Tut..tut..tut . . . now look what you've done," he scolded, "You've let him escape."

" I'm sorry, mister . . . I didna mean to . . ."

"You're a naughty girl. I'll have to spank you," he said, smiling as if he didn't mean it, his eyelid pulsing rapidly.

She was lifted effortlessly into the air and taken under his arm to a nearby shed. He sat in an old chair and dumped her, face down, across his knee. She didn't like the smell. She started flailing her arms and legs around, squealing to be free.

"Now, now, now, . . . you mustn't," he said, " I have to punish you for letting the bunny out."

Ruthie had been spanked before. She gritted her teeth in expectation of the thrashing as her knickers were pulled down to the ankles. The large hand smacked down on her backside, fingers lingering on pink exposed skin. He began to rock her body against his rough trousers. Smack went the hand again, harder this time, making her cry out "Chrissie! . . . Help, Chrissie!"

She flinched as his fingers stroked her thighs, then rhythmically squeezed her buttocks, before feeling roughly between her legs. The sensations were strange, not like any punishment she'd ever had before. The man was moaning now, rocking her faster. He started to fumble with his trouser buttons. Ruthie wet herself, feeling the urine run hot over her belly, wetting his breeks. This would make him furious, she thought, screaming now in terror: "Mammy, mammy, mammy . . ."

Suddenly, Chrissie burst through the shed door. Her reactions were instinctive, fast, frenzied. Her voice was full of venom: "Leave m' sister alone, ye dirty bugger!"

She thumped the hefty marrow bone against his head and pulled Ruth from his lap, her knickers trailing. Before he recovered, they had gone. Over her shoulder, Chrissie yelled: "I ken who ye are! I'll fetch m' dad! I'll fetch the bobbies!"

The lump of boiling beef lay on the floor, spoilt.

CHAPTER
22

Pain, Pleasure and Parting

Johnie accompanied Tom Hepburn on his mission. He had tried to persuade Tom to go through the official channels but, having reported the incident to the police, who documented it and said they would "look into it", the wheels of justice seemed much too slow for the enraged father. He could not contain himself. He stormed into the moneylender's premises. Silas was in the front shop, counting the day's takings from the till and carefully stacking neat piles of coins into a drawer before deigning to look up. He peered at them over the rim of tortoise-shelled spectacles. Recognising Johnie, but ignoring the presence of his red faced companion, he said:

"I told you last month, boy . . . I am not prepared to do business with you . . . or any of your kind."

"We're here on business of anither kind, Mr. Smith..." Johnie began. He was cut short by Tom's voice. He shouted the words as if to compensate for his own deafness: "Aye, mister . . . a bad business . . . Ye can keep yer bloody money! We've come to get a hold o' yer dirty brute of a son . . .and tak him tae the jailhoose . . . an' I hope he rots 'ere . . . fur whit he's done tae m'quinie!" Tom said more, spitting out the gist of the sorry story with his anger making him almost inarticulate.

Silas's face blanched. He said nothing. He took his glasses off and looked exposed, naked, miserable. After a silence, he said quietly: "I don't know where he is . . . he didn't come back to work this afternoon . . . he's not at home either . . . his mother is worried."

Harold Smith had vanished.

Johnie led Tom from the dingy shop. Silas Smith had taken the confrontation very calmly. Surely, he must have been aware that something was very wrong with the boy? Perhaps he had suspicions but had not realised the extent of the problem? After all, the youth had simply appeared quiet and reserved to people visiting the shop . . . a little persecuted by his father perhaps. Johnie had imagined that

131

it would be gratifying to confront and mortify this prejudiced man. However, he experienced no sweetness in this kind of revenge. He felt only empathy for Silas and pity for his son.

That night, Jean had trouble sleeping. She was plagued by nightmares as the weight of tragedy pressed on her being like an iron yoke. The colour was leached out of her by fatigue and her eyes were sunk deep into dark sockets. As the days passed, however, her despair was gradually infiltrated by an inner rage. She bottled up this anger and the grief. She could not cry.

Frequently, she got up at six and went for a walk, always taking the same route: up Burgh Road and down towards the Sletts, inexplicably drawn to the sea. Sometimes her feet took her to the graveyard at the Knab but this particular day, she walked along the rocky shore path, south towards Sound and Clickimin. She was thinking about Willie . . . He had become a regular and welcome visitor, a lifeline in her grey life. His voice had developed a hoarseness and he seemed to be pained with indigestion although he never complained of his own troubles. They were well matched at a game of chess, Willie being surprised and delighted that she had learnt the game. She looked forward to the sessions as a therapeutic detour from reality, requiring logical thought and no emotion. She did not have to think about painful matters, only to apply her inbuilt powers of reason from first principles . . . a process that was undemanding and much preferable to real life.

It was still dark. There was a full moon, a clear starry sky. The footpath was deserted. Large frothy breakers rumbled up over the Sletts pier and the beam of the Bressay lighthouse fell across the undulating swell. There was a figure, she thought, standing right out at the point of the flat rocky platform. It was there one minute . . . and gone the next.

She wrapped her coat more tightly around her. She felt chilled. The cold sensation quickly changing to one of fear . . . hope . . . disbelief. Salt spray battered her cheeks and blurred her vision . . . but she was sure. She ran to the place. There was a glimpse of shining black hair . . . a body floating face down. Instinctively, she threw off her coat and shoes and jumped. She was a good swimmer and knew this shoreline well. She grasped the limp figure and hauled it to the

132

waterline, dragging it to a gulley of shingle, assisted by the tide flow. The body was still.

She knew what to do in such circumstances. Yet, she hesitated . . . It was the Smith boy, the one who'd . . .! She choked on a sick disgust, reluctant to begin artificial respiration but driven by conscience. She tilted his head back and checked the airway for obstruction. Water ran from his mouth. Then she shut her eyes as she pressed down on the ribcage, and then pulled the arms upwards and outwards, counting out the rhythmn. After several repeats, the chest coughed its way back to the world of the living . . . to a weird world where a strange woman was bent overhead and shouting: "It's nae fair . . . it's nae fair!"

Jean behaved mechanically, her thoughts out of sympathy with her actions. She did not understand why God should take the good and innocent from her and then use her as an instrument for resurrecting evil.

———

Unexpectedly, Willie came to Lerwick that afternoon to attend an auction. He intended to buy some wood to build a garage workshop for Billy who would be home by Christmas and would need a starting place for rehabilitation, a safe base to practise his engineering skills and hopefully regain the use of his injured hand. Agnes had quizzed Willie more than usual about this trip. It was becoming obvious that his visits into town were uncharacteristically frequent. He had showed her the advertisement in the Shetland Times:

"WOOD FOR SALE.
    I will sell by auction, on 30 October, at 4 o'clock in the afternoon, a quantity of timber, suitable for the erection of fishworkers' houses.
                            Frank J. Smith,
                                Auctioneer."

This had satisfied her for the time being. He had told her not to worry if he was late getting back.

He had no hesitation in bidding on some appropriate lots of timber, and by tea-time he was at Parkfield Road. Jean was sitting in the dark. It had been a terrible day. Since the morning's trauma, she had been unable to stop weeping. She had not been a model witness when the police inspector and a female colleague came to interview her in the afternoon. It was the first time since the funeral that she had really cried and her face was swollen purple by the time Willie arrived. Muttering apologies, she got up to wash her face and put the kettle on. There was a faltering in her voice as she told him the story. He was first astonished and then aghast. He felt her bitter hurt and longed to share her burden.

The fire was well down. He sat beside the dying embers and riddled the ashes, causing a little flurry of halfhearted flames. He placed a shovelful of new coals, listening to the hiss as the damp lumps met hot cinders. It was a cold night outside and inside he was chilled. He felt the bonemarrow aching in his extremities and pulled his boots off, holding his stocking feet to the weak source of warmth.

She was in a dwaam as she brought him some tea. As she passed the cup to him, he instinctively put his cold hand over hers and held it for a second. Her tears, still very close to the surface, came again in a flood of grateful emotion for this gentle, caring, wordless action. She needed human contact. He put his tea on the hearth and rose. He pulled her close to him and held her, loving her and knowing he had no right to make this known. His heart pounded against his ribs and he longed for the circumstances of their lives to be different. He wanted to make love, to blot out her pain and smother it in pleasure, but he was content just to hold her.

Jean's thoughts were erratic. She knew that her hormone balance was abnormal following the miscarriage and that she was in a poor mental and physical state. However, she responded fiercely to the touch of this man who had become so dear to her. She needed to be held. Tears trickled down her face and her nose ran. It did not matter." Shhh . . . it's all right, lass. Let it go," he murmured, as sobs shuddered in her thin frame.

She did not want to move and clung to her comforter. He was warm while the unjust world outside was cold and dark and empty. She inhaled his familiar soothing smell and she was suddenly aware of his body. It was totally unexpected, a rapid burning awakening, hot and hungry. She had been like a dead empty shell since she lost the child but she was now alive. Her problems ceased to exist, there was only this man. It was her voice that broke the silence, speaking words full of urgency:

"God, Willie, I need ye so much . . . Please, Willie . . . Stay wi' me tonight . . ."

"A'll bide as lang as du needs me, lass, but dinna act hasty, du's no deesel . . . The least said and done, the shunest

134

mended." As he spoke, a sudden impulse responded to her heat and he pressed her to him, knowing that this was unfair in her present state of mind, but he loved her . . . he loved her.

Never had her physical longing been so overwhelming. The sharp thrill of arousal swamped her. She did not want to control it. She raised a stained face to his and telling eyes met. He caressed her cheeks, tasting warm salty tears and pressing his lips to her forehead. She kissed him full on the mouth . . . and there was no more stopping.

The two became as one, their private hidden wounds forgotten as they tumbled through a one way tunnel of dazzling pleasure while shades of steely grey were locked outside. She heard endearments from his heart. There was no inhibition or shame. She knew that he loved her dearly and was glad that his hands and mind were sure in their maturity. She abandoned herself to the sensations and heard herself call out as she reached the very peak of ecstasy for the first time in her life. His dampness mingled with hers.

She cried and laughed in pain and joy and gratitude. He talked reassuringly, rocking her in his arms like a child, stroking her hair till she slept.

In a happy delirious state, he stayed till the dawn started to break, admiring her sleeping form again and again in disbelief. His mind whirled in fearful turmoil. How could he spend his remaining days with her? How would he deal with Agnes? There was no solution. Yet he would not change this night to save his soul.

When she woke, she found a sheet of paper lying by the bedside:

"Jeanie,
> *I love dee in a hunder wyes -*
> *Ah'll nemm but een or twa.*
> *I love dee laek da simmer sun*
> *Dat drives da cloods awa.*
> *I love dee as da dearest freend,*
> *Dis weary wirld can shaa,*
> *I love dee as my sweethert,*
> *Till sleep an shadows faa.*
> *Da lass dat lyghts my wirld o dremms,*
> *Da star dat ootshines aa.*

She felt a lump in her throat and knew then that this

happiness was doomed to be short-lived. Calm now in the clear light of morning, she examined what had occurred.

It was wrong. It could never be. Willie had a wife . . . James was barely cold in his grave. She knew that she must break all ties. She cared deeply. She owed him so much for allaying her despair, for his comfort and strength. She must now rebuild her life on her own strength, not on the wreckage of his family, Billy Leask's family . . . it was barely credible!

James had left her nothing but a share in the boat. Rather than sell to a stranger, Johnie had persuaded her to allow him to buy, paying her a little each week, enough to cover her rent and food. She must look for work before she was destitute.

She resolved there and then to leave Shetland. She had an address for Jennifer. She would leave on the St. Rognvald right away.

Willie came in the afternoon, unable to stay away. She told him immediately. He frowned but said nothing. He understood. Anyway, what had he to offer her? A few short months, probably, and then she'd be alone again. He wrestled briefly with his conscience . . . to tell her about his illness . . . to appeal to her sympathy and keep her near . . . No, he did not want her to watch his deterioration as the disease wasted him. It was best that she find a new start . . . and a new love. The thought confused him and he drew her towards him in a tight hug.

They loved each other slowly and gently that afternoon, the blinds drawn and the door locked against the unfairness of the world. Warm velvet darkness enveloped them, like the soft secret lining inside a trinket box. Their union was beautiful.

Before he left, he added another verse to the poem:

> "Da day is come when we man pairt,
> Wir gyaets may seldom meet,
> An yit ah'll tink o' dee, my lass
> An keep dee in me hert
> Until du comes agenn ta me,
> Whan mirk nyght closes in,
> Ta lyght da wye we aa mann tak
> An pit dee haand in mine."

He drove home in the darkness and tears of rain

136

streamed down his windscreen. He cared not for the wrath of Agnes that awaited him...it was a small price to pay. His wife was suspicious, certainly, but likely she assumed that his illness was affecting his character and causing these strange nocturnal habits.

He did not sleep. He walked the floor. The pain was bad and he took morphia. He wrote his thoughts in the notebook:

> " Du's gyaain shune, my Jeanie,
> So whit care I whit weary Time may bring?
> Ee day athoot wan wird, wan smile,
> Or waarmin glance fae saft broon een,
> Drees oot in langsome weariness,
> As grey cloods greyer hing,
> Ower darkening hills and sky.
> Da mirkness closes in
> Whan du is far fae me.
> Yet still a braeth, a touch
> Live on in hert an memory.
> Whan du is geen
> Sae shune may I be tu."

Knowing that his will to fight the cancer was weakened, he made plans to fetch Billy home early. He would go South to the hospital. They would release his son to him as a doctor as well as a father. He had much to do. He was needed by his patients and his son. He must not feel sorry for himself.

In Parkfield Road, Jean was packing. She wept. She would say goodbye to her mother and the rest of her family tomorrow . . .and leave the island that had become her home. An inner voice chanted "Holm, sweet holm". . . it was not a happy home.

23

Seeking a New Start

The seventeen hour trip to Aberdeen was a smooth one. Jean stood on deck watching the moonlight on the water and staring up at the vast myriads of twinkling stars. She focused on the three stars of Orion's belt. Willie's cheerful voice came into her mind, "Da leddy ell-waand" he called this array. He had taught her Shetland names for many of the familiar constellations. It was like learning a new language.

The ocean looked peaceful and beautiful, lying quietly like a sleeping giant but she knew it could be merciless, full of wrath and fury. Life-giving, it nurtured millions of marine forms and yet a hungry life-taker too. Her father and James were near her now, she felt.

She strained her eyes into the bodiless darkness and shivered, afraid. She felt a tap on her shoulder. Startled, she turned to see a woman. In the light from a porthole, Jean recognised Mrs Silas Smith. Her eyes were red-rimmed and puffy. She grasped Jean's hand and said:

"Thank you again, Mrs West . . . He's all I have, despite his sins. He's sick, you see."

"It's aa right, I understand, Mrs Smith."

We have a strange tragic bond, Jean thought, her and I. We have suffered loss. We are unable to salve our heartaches. The sea murmured and the ship's engines throbbed keeping time with their heartbeat. Jean patted the woman's hand. For a while they lent together on the railings deriving some solace from each other's silence.

Later, she told Jean that her son had been assessed and was now on board, under the supervision of a police doctor, on his way to Cornhill Asylum, where he would receive the best of care and treatment. She was going to live nearby for a while. Jean listened quietly. The phosphorescence that glinted like treasure in the bow wave caught her eye . . . so many marine micro-organisms. She remembered Willie saying that there were many people with psychiatric problems. Regional Medical Records indicated that more than thirty were registered as "insane" in Shetland.

However, this represented an incidence of less than 1 in 1000, while Scotland as a whole had more than double that frequency, about 1 in 400.

When the woman had gone below deck, the air seemed suddenly colder and Jean became aware of dark premonitions she had felt before. She rubbed the goosepimples on her tightly crossed arms. She flinched as her hand touched a bruise on her rib. Perhaps she'd hurt it during those private hours with Willie. Yet, she did not recollect bumping into anything. Was he in some sort of pain? She only wished she knew.

Jennifer made her welcome. She laughed and hugged her and could not stop talking. Jean learned all about the terrible accident at the factory where her friend had been badly burned including her beautiful hair and part of her face. She had spent two months in hospital but she was almost fully recovered now. The scars were not bad, just shiny and smooth with none of the lived-in character of real skin. Sometimes the burn marks were a bit livid, but she was an expert at disguising them, using chalk to tone the colour down.

As a patient at Glasgow Royal Infirmary, Jennifer had taken a great interest in the work of the nurses and had consequently enrolled as a trainee after her discharge. There she had met Robert Jenkins, a convalescing serviceman. He had been gassed and still had an asthmatic wheeze. They were to be married soon, she told Jean. Despite trying hard to restrain herself, Jean cried. It took some time to tell her own tragic story. Jennifer wept too.

The flat was tiny, but there was room enough for friends, Jennifer insisted. "Stay as long as you like, Jean. You've been through a lot lately and I've got so much happiness. Share a little of it with me. It is small, but Robert has his own house, and I'll be moving there when we marry. You could keep this place on, if you like."

"I'll need work, Jenny"

"Well, why not try nursing? They're still looking for trainees, especially now that the VAD's have mostly gone home. I could introduce you to the matron, she'll know."

Within a few weeks Jean started nursing. She was surprised that some of the work turned her stomach. After being elbow deep in fish guts for much of her life, she assumed that she would be immune to all odours but human sick smells were overpowering! She emptied bedpans, cleaned sluices, and, as training progressed, changed dressings from all sorts of weeping wounds. There were still a few patients being transferred to the hospital from abroad with lingering war injuries: burns and gas gangrene. The latter type of lesion was particularly repulsive since it swelled with putrid gas and needed washing out every day. It was clearly painful for the sufferer and she herself had to hold her breath to stem the nausea. However, one young man retained a sense of humour despite his plight. Jean encouraged bantering.

"Foo's the gammy knee today then, George?"

"Hurts like hell, nurse, and smells like shit! It's all that horse manure the Frogs put on to Flanders' fields that's got into me leg, I reckon."

"It's got into yer heed as weel, I think! . . . Come on, drop yer breeks."

"Anytime, nurse, when's your day off?"

She enjoyed this light-hearted teasing. She developed a real rapport with the patients, often stopping to chat, or to play a game of cards or chess, at the close of her shift. She had nothing to hurry back for. She always accepted overtime. It made her feel needed and useful and, in some short measure, fulfilled. Yet, at night in bed, she was lonely and the emptiness was a part of her life.

She felt dizzy and sick less often as she adjusted to the nursing duties. She was glad now that she had forced herself to persevere when she had actually vomited a few times in the early weeks. Then, suddenly and incredibly, a strange truth dawned on her. It was Jennifer who first hinted at it. They were trying on wedding dresses and Jean, a maid of honour, was having trouble with the hooks and eyes at the waistline of her dress.

"Aye, Jenny, Glasgow certainly agrees with me, I'm putting on the inches all right!"

"Oh yes," laughed the other, "or maybe you're carrying another bairn, eh?"

The words silenced her for a full minute.

"No. No, it canna be 'at" she said, slowly. A trace of wrinkles wreathed her brow. "It canna be!"

"When did you last have your courses?"

Jean did her sums. She was loath to accept the right answer.

"Weel, nae since I lost the baby . . . but I bled for mair'n

140

three weeks then, so I expect my body is still adjusting to normal."

"You should see the doctor, Jeanie, you have that maternal look, honestly! I've a trained eye for such things, remember."

A letter from home came every few weeks, usually from Johnie, occasionally with small contributions from the others tagged on as postscripts. Jean was always eager for their news.

It was the start of a new season and gutters wages were up: arles £2; £1 per week basic pay with 10p per barrel extra . . . getting better, but still poor, she thought. The Disposal Board had sold some of the stockpiled herrings to Russia at 35/- a barrel, so a few trade routes were opening up. However, the fishermen feared another poor season. They blamed whaling for the decline in herring stocks to the west of Shetland, although they were having difficulty obtaining direct evidence. Johnie was actively involved in the anti-whaling faction and was participating in local meetings with the council. In an effort to urge legislation to prohibit the activity, they were even considering sending a deputation to the Secretary of State for Scotland! Jean was impressed.

She was also concerned to learn that her mother was unwell, thin with a racking cough that had lingered for several weeks.

She worked well into her seventh month of pregnancy, saving every penny. She wrote to Johnie and asked him to buy out her share of the Prosperity immediately. She did not tell him why she needed money and he did not ask, but he managed to raise the funds. The vessel was living up to her name, his next letter said. She had been fitted with a diesel engine and had developed a reputation for good catches. He had studied his father's detailed personal charts, drawn up before the war and kept as rough pencil drawings in the back of his logbook. He had surprised the rest of the crew with an uncanny knowledge of the meads that resulted in successful hauls time and time again. It was more essential than ever to maximise gross earnings since overheads had gone up four-fold over the pre-war costs, due to the growing use of motor engines.

In July 1920, Jean gave birth to a healthy baby boy. She marvelled at the living part of herself and gingerly stroked the downy head, awash with love as she breast fed. She doted on the infant. She had found happiness at last, in fact 8lb 10oz of happiness, a very big baby for a slip of a woman, the midwife had said, and beautiful too. She told nobody at home about him. She was scared that if she spoke of "Alan William", he might be snatched away by the same malevolent force that was responsible for all the other tragedies in her life. Here, he was safe, yet she longed to show him off with pride to Johnie, to his grandmother, to his great-grandmother, to his father, to the world.

Thus she joined the ranks of the unmarried mothers. Glasgow teemed with them, like every other city in the country. Alan was not a war baby but the circumstances were maybe similar. She had picked up a pamphlet in the maternity waiting-room, entitled "Story of a Girl's Soul", published in support of the Mission of Hope Homes for unmarried mothers and their children:

"There came an hour when the youth pleaded and the girl yielded. She does not blame him. It is part of her honesty to tell you honestly that the fault was hers as much as his. She does not say "He tempted me". She says that for both of them the pressure of temptation was too strong, and that in a moment of sheer unconscious tumult of mind and heart the thing happened which was to wreck her youth."

The words struck a chord of understanding . . . except for the last line. The thing had happened and it was wonderful. She had made a new start from the wreck of youth.

CHAPTER
24
Tinkin Lang fur Dee

November 11, 1920, the second anniversary of Armistice
day, saw Billy Leask's business begin to pick up. Starting
initially from a small wooden garage based in Whiteness, he
had adjusted to his physical handicaps and remained a first
class engineer. Soon, he had found a partner in Lerwick and
between them they had established a successful garage and
workshop. The time was right for this kind of enterprise,
since motor engines were becoming indispensable in all kinds
of workplaces: butchers; bakers; barrel factories; feed-stuff
dealers; cabinet makers; saw-mills; laundry works; printing
works; hotels; iron works; farms (for threshing etc.); fishing
boat engines; foghorns in lighthouses; not to mention cars
and motor-cycles.

Billy had originally thought that it might be best to
specialise in boat engines, but his partner, Michael, had
persuaded him that a general business servicing cars and
bikes was a more sensible approach. Michael understood
current and imminent requirements in Shetland. He saw
that there was considerable competition already in marine
engineering, with several small firms setting up as local
agents for larger concerns in the south. Walter Duncan from
Hamnavoe was a good example, an accredited dealer in
Gardner engines or John R. Barclay in Mid Yell, specialising
in Kelvins. Furthermore, there was a lack of hard cash
around for boat conversions, despite the well-intentioned
promises of local and national government.

Michael was a shrewd businessman, basing his estimates
on statistics. He studied the breakdown of vessel types in
Lerwick harbour: 25% had motor engines; 35% were steam
driven; and the majority, about 40%, were still under
antiquated sail, struggling now to make a living.
Furthermore, the past fishing season had been poor partly
due to a scarcity of herring and partly to the uncertain
European markets. As a temporary measure, the government
had baled out the curers by agreeing to buy the summer's
herring surplus. The industry remained depressed. Against

this background, it was obvious to him that the conversion and reconditioning of sail ships would be a slow process.

By comparison, the motor car trade was expanding rapidly. The first garage had opened in Lerwick even before the war. Now there were several firms conducting sales and transport services throughout Shetland: P. Solotti & Sons, Ganson's, among others in Lerwick; several hire firms like James Hay in Brae and Tulloch & Son in the West Mainland. Limited passenger services now operated throughout the rural areas.

"It's the transport of the future, Billy," he said. "Already there are almost as many around as there are horse-drawn vehicles. Plenty people in this town can easily afford £35 for a new BSA motor cycle . . . or even £465 for a new Buick. Look at the speed of travel. Why, last week, two folk were fined for speeding on the Esplanade . . . one of them was doing nearly twenty miles an hour. Compare that to a horse."

Michael was right, of course. Their business venture fortuitously coincided with a phase of exponential growth in the use of engines on land. The council's vice-convener was quoted in the press as saying: "I think the people of Lerwick have lost the use of their legs altogether." However, the growth at sea was slower.

Billy's homecoming had boosted his father's failing spirits. Willie had been inexplicably depressed and ailing during the autumn of 1919, but he had shown a definite improvement over the Christmas period and through to the Spring. During this brief remission, he had been pleased to see his family together for the first time in years and also thankfully preoccupied with helping his son to establish his business. However, he had relapsed that summer. By July, the severity of his condition was apparent to his family and his patients. He had lost much weight and looked grey and wasted, like a skeleton with skin. His teeth and cheekbones had become prominent and the chicken sinews of premature ageing showed on his neck. He had to hold his trousers up with braces because he could not bear a tight belt. He was clearly in pain for much of the time, despite careful use of self administered drugs. Thus, he was eventually forced to give warning of his intention to quit practise, so allowing time for the recruitment of an emergency replacement for the area.

Willie read the notice that appeared in "The Shetland Times" in early November:

"Wanted.

A medical officer and public vaccinator for the Parish of Tingwall, Whiteness and Weisdale, to take up duties immediately. The annual salary will be £45 including cost of medicines and dressings.

Applications and testimonials to be lodged with the subscriber by the end of the month.

David Beatton,
Inspector of Poor of Tingwall."

Willie laid the newspaper down with a sigh and leant his head in his hands. He bit his lip against an internal discomfort and retreated into his thoughts. Fond memories helped him get by when things were bleak. He had promised himself that he would not intrude on Jean's life ever again. However, as he moped, the certain knowledge that he would be dead by Christmas was uppermost in his mind. He longed to see her one more time.

His private notebook was locked away in his medical bag. He picked up a pen and paper and wrote in shaky Norwegian:

"Ensome.

> *Hvor er du na, min elskling?*
> *Til; evig tid i sjelen min,*
> *Alltid i mine drommer.*
> *Reis hvor som helsk du vil,*
> *Men komm til sist til meg.*
> *Dagene er triste, og jeg lengter*
> *Etter deg, som gleder meg i diamanter*
> *Eller himmelrikes sjerner.*
> *Ensom er jeg*
> *Nar du er langt fra meg,*
> *Og ode livets lyst."*

He read it through and the sheer emotion of his own invention touched his heart and made tears prick at his eyes. On a fresh sheet, he translated it into his native words, put it into an envelope and addressed it to Jean, c/o Mrs Mary Watt, at 4, Klondyke Cottages. She might never receive it, he thought. Should others read it, they would never know who had sent it.

He posted it, regretting the deed immediately. Yet, in his contradictory heart . . . he hoped.

25
Reaching Out

A letter from Johnie came at the end of November. Jean read it avidly, the news from home, in sheet upon sheet: ...Mary was worse, coughing continuously now and hiding her bloodstained hankerchiefs...possible signs of consumption . . . Jean was missed at home . . . Jessie was doing well at school and there was talk of a scholarship . . . Johnie had a girlfriend, Isobel . . . David had speared a 6ft 9in fluke in the north harbour and had sold it to a local dealer for £4 15/- . . . the incident had attracted a lot of attention when he had jumped out of the boat to haul the monster up the slip...it had even been reported in the local paper . . . a new electric machine was being pioneered in Lerwick – it threatened women's jobs since it could split 2300 herrings an hour using a revolving circular knife . . .

There was another envelope enclosed. Jean's heart missed a beat as she recognised the familiar handwriting. She felt a stab of pain in her side as she opened it:

"Tinkin lang fur dee.

> *Whaar is du noo, my ain dear love?*
> *Forever i me heart,*
> *Aye ita me dremms.*
> *Geeng whaare'er du will,*
> *But come in life's huimin ta me.*
> *Da days are dreich an I tink lang*
> *For dee at maks me blyder still*
> *Dan aa da riches o da aert*
> *An da starns in heeven abuin.*
> *Lonly am I*
> *Whan du is far fae me:*
> *A wastelaand, life's desires."*

No signature. His gentleness came wafting into her being, a warm breath. Then she felt his immediacy, his pulsating presence . . . a vibrating hum, a beat of urgency . . . "But

come in life's huimin ta me." She knew then that he was
dying and that she must go home. He needed her and he had
a right to see his son.

She looked tenderly at little Alan, sleeping peacefully,
with his father's dimple sweetly and innocently displayed on
his chin.

CHAPTER
26
So Near

The boat journey was wearisome and Jean spent the choppy passage on deck, a little uneasy about the reception that might await her. She was able to catch up on the local news, having borrowed a Shetland Times from the purser . . . There were plans to build a slipway at the Malakoff, that would be the first dry-dock facility on the island. Rules and regulations were being drafted to govern the fish stalls at Alexandra wharf – a good thing, she thought, since standards of hygiene were less than desirable. There were several angry letters from readers about fishcuring at the Knab, which was seen as a sacrosanct recreational area for the Town, not to be exploited by fisherfolk who should be banished to the north end. Jean was sad to glean that the Scottie colony was still resented and isolated. She turned to the "Sunday Corner." The texts were far from reassuring:

" *Sin is like a river which begins in a quiet spring and ends in a tumultuous sea.*"

" *There are no means of escape from the cells of a guilty conscience.*"

"*Responsibility must be shouldered; you cannot carry it under your arm.*"

The Atora suet recipe was a more promising source of comfort – a rich clooty dumpling, she'd try it when she got home. She discarded the newspaper.

She had developed more self-confidence from her nursing job and her year of independence and she felt that she could deal with the difficulties ahead. However, she was also wary of many memories that milled in her mind as the boat advanced into the south entrance of Lerwick harbour. It was a bleak raw morning, dreary grey mist shrouding the sleeping town. The seagulls were nostalgically noisy and the taste of salt spray was both invigorating and sad. Her mood relaxed, though, as the familiar landmarks materialised in welcome. The Market Cross, the Town Hall, sprawling lines of slumbering herring stations, their barrels stacked high. Home, she thought, . . . holm sweet holm.

The boat's whistle brayed sonorously across the sound. Alan, who had been asleep in her arms, whimpered into wakefulness. She lifted him high in the air, suddenly exhilarated:

"We're hame, wee fellow. We're hame!" The shock of it all made him girn. This was a cold, alien place. He did not share her enthusiasm.

Like a puppy or a fluffy kitten, the exuberance of babyhood quickly overcame the initial shock and resentment. He gurgled at his strange new relatives as if he'd known them all his short life. He was not backward, but trusting, warm and friendly. Barely six months, he almost had words and he was certainly able to make his feelings known. Although Jean refused to answer any questions about him, the cute dimple was a striking trait, evoking strong suspicions about the identity of his father. Although Jean was not shunned by her family, there were a few whispered comments and snide remarks overheard in the community. She was called "Scottie slut" and "whoring fishwife." She endured her shame with a calm dignity and busied herself nursing her mother. It was still crowded at home with her other brothers and sisters now taking up teenage space.

A few days later, she caught the Westside transport bus to visit Willie, wondering what on earth she would say if his wife answered the door. She left the child at home with Elsie, considering it best to introduce him gradually.

The bus left from just outside Islesburgh House in King Harald Street. She made an arrangement with the driver to pick her up on the return trip, giving her about two hours. She was nervous now and felt like abandoning the idea, but the poignant words of a poem echoed in her mind and she took a seat.

She smoothed her skirt and fiddled with her hair. She had dressed carefully in her best grey wool suit, a cream blouse with a high mandarin-type neckline and a little cameo brooch at the collar. The suit fitted well and she wore a soft wool hat to match, two shades darker, a cream braid detail at the brim. She looked older, more mature. She was aware of a tiny cold sore on her upper lip, barely noticeable to anyone else, but on fire with the burning sensation that heralded a week of the trivial but unsightly affliction. What caused these things anyway, she pondered. A girl at school had once told her it was a spider's pee, but she was not aware of any recent spider being close enough to urinate on her lip . . . and why did it cluster in the same place all the time? . . . Ah well, Willie wouldn't care.

The journey went so quickly that she scarcely noticed the passing countryside. It was a bright, frosty day, with little wind, a freak pleasure for early December. The fields lay bare yet the weak rays of sunshine somehow added intricate colour to this drab winter sward. Shades of brown, mossy green, gold, yellow ochre and wine red dappled bright across smooth bare hillsides . . . like the autumn leaves on trees in the south, she thought. She had a sudden wish that she could paint this shifting scene that was so simple and beautiful . . . so typical of Shetland.

She walked up the path to the heavy door with its oversized knocker. She rapped purposefully. Her heart thumped. Margaret answered. Clearly she had no idea who Jean was.

"Yes, can I help you?" she said, puzzled.

"I was wondering if I could possibly have a word with Dr. Leask? I'm an auld friend of his . . . Jean West."

"I am sorry but I really dinna think he is up tae having visitors . . . You see, my faider is very ill." Her voice quavered.

Jean spoke softly: "Margaret, isn't it? I am sure that Dr. Leask would want tae see me . . . Could you possibly tell him I'm here?"

"We.eel, I'll go and ask mam, but I doobt if she will agree tae it. What wis da name again?"

Jean could hear a rasping querulous voice within. She shut her eyes tight and her stomach fluttered in anticipation.

Margaret, pale faced, came back. She was apologetic but firm: " I'm afraid she will no allow onybody tae see him. I dinna ken your business wi' my faider, but your presence has clearly upset mam. I must ask you no tae come back. I'm sorry."

Jean stood, stupefied and deeply rooted to the porch step, like a docken.

"In 'at case, will you at least tell me if he is able to speak? . . . He's not in pain, is he?"

"He is dying, Mrs West. He is as weel as can be expected in dat condition."

"Please tell him that I came. He would want to ken 'at."

The door clunked shut with finality. Willie lay unreachable within, Jean unwelcome without. It was impossible. She could write. Would her letter be intercepted?

150

It was too chancy. She waited nearby for the next few minutes, silently willing her presence to be felt. Then she walked away.

Suddenly, she remembered Willa, the old woman. She turned with renewed purpose towards Willa's crofthouse.

She found her in the dim-lit barn, and almost fainted when she fathomed the scene. A sheep hung from a hook, the throat cut, the lifeblood dripping into a pail on the earthen floor. A smothered youthful dream pierced her senses. As the old one turned, it was Willie's face that she saw.

"My, my lass, what ails dee!" Willa cried, waddling anxiously towards this unexpected visitor who stood silent, like a wraith.

"But du's da wife at nearly hed dee bairn here twa year back, isn't du? Yis, yis, I ken dee noo. I never forgit a boanny face. Come du in bye tae da fire, lass."

She ushered Jean into the little house, reeky with peat smoke. She yattered away, apparently oblivious to her guest's rapt stupor.

CHAPTER
27
Holm Again

A short letter came three days later:

"Dear Jean,
Willie is gone. The funeral is on Monday. I don't think
Agnes would want you at the wake. Willie hated funerals -
men marching in black suits and starched collars, the starch
spreading up over their faces.
I got your message to him. He smiled and said you are not
to grieve. He asked me to put twartree peerie mussel pearls in
his pocket. I have done his bidding. God rest his soul.
Willa Leask."

Jean did not attend the funeral. That afternoon, she
walked . . . through Parkfield Road, past the house where
Alan had been conceived, and she was vexed that Willie had
never known about his son. She touched the lintel of the
ground floor room as she passed, sadness sensitive in her
fingers, the ghosts of James and her stillborn daughter. It
was a cold day. She was disinclined to loiter.

She went on, past the Hillhead site earmarked for the war
memorial. It was to be a grand symbol of remembrance,
£2,000 for the architect's fees alone, she'd read, and much of
the cost contributed by the fishing industry. She continued
over the Knab, recalling their walks together, his laughter
ringing in her ears, love filling her heart. She passed the
place where she had rescued the youth. She wondered what
became of him. The area had already changed. New houses
had appeared on Knab Road, Breiwick Road, Ronald Street,
and at the extremities of King Harald Street and St. Olaf
Street. Johnie and Isobel had applied for one of these council
houses. The rents were reasonable, at £15 a year for three
rooms, but demand outstripped supply. Johnie grumbled that
maybe his surname had not helped placement on the waiting
list.

By the time she returned home, she had decided that she
would go to Willie's grave to pay her private last

respects...but not yet . . . in the springtime, when the mayflowers came, when the family visits were likely to be done and fewer people were around.

Yule was a happier time. It was Alan's first Christmas and he thrived on the attention and the excitement, although he was more preoccupied with the coloured wrapping papers than the presents.

Her mother improved a little and Jean tried to get a nursing job, but these positions were invariably full time or live-in. Unemployment was high in the town, with 226 men, 10 women, 8 boys and 3 girls registered. After applying to numerous advertisements, she obtained a few hours casual work as a maid in the sanatorium. She supplemented this meagre income by knitting fair isle hosery for sale to J.R. White. It was while she was taking a batch of garments to Commercial Street that she caught her first glimpse of Billy. He was driving past, talking to a woman passenger, whom she could not see clearly. Perhaps he had a wife. She enquired at the woolshop about the young man in the motor car. They confirmed that it was Billy Leask, a successful businessman with engineering premises at Garthspool. From that day, she avoided going near that particular area. In fact, she became a bit of a recluse. With the exception of attending her work, she seldom ventured far from the immediate vicinity of the house and went shopping only in the late afternoon, under cover of winter darkness.

With such a solitary lifestyle, she did not expect to acquire a suitor. Gordon Clarke was a teacher from the Central School, whom she met through her sister Jessie, a star pupil in his English class. She had gone to the school in place of her mother, who remained chronically ill (and still persistently refused to set a foot inside that awesome place), to discuss the possibility of a scholarship which would allow Jessie to continue her education beyond the age of fourteen. This had not proved financially possible. Even with the help of a bursary, the family could not afford higher education, especially knowing the fees quoted for a university degree: 45 guineas for an M.A. and 90 guineas for a B.Sc. Nevertheless, Jean had been quite impressed with the dominie's authority and sincerity. He showed no bias towards the Scotties.

He was sitting in his office, fenced in by an imposing desk. His voice was deep, one that demanded undivided attention. She sensed a keen humour underlying the austere

153

professional surface and he clearly cared about his scholars. He had a reputation for being dedicated with a fine teaching ability. She was attracted right away and they clicked into an easy-going relationship. He was in his early thirties and obviously enjoyed edible pursuits, a fact reflected in his physique: the pudding belly that sagged comfortably below the belt of his trousers, the lirks of soft flesh between gaping shirt buttons when he dared to laugh or relax, the criss-cross patterns of port-drinker's veins on his nose and the purple complexion of high blood pressure. Still, he was jolly and amusing. He gave a feeling of security and was good company.

Gordon first asked her to accompany him to a charity concert in the Town Hall, where the famous Miss Helen Ford, a mezzo/contralto, gave a stunning performance. It was in aid of the Gilbert Bain Hospital and Missions to Fishgirls. Jean was surprised that she enjoyed the evening so much. Gordon did not care for pastimes as energetic as dancing. Instead, they went occasionally to the North Star Cinema. They saw "The Town of Crooked Ways", starring Poppy Wyndham, a plot set in an idyllic Yorkshire village. Perhaps, in a fairytale setting like that, she might have lived with Gordon, feeling contented, but there was no passion. He also took her to see "The Thinker", a powerful drama about an artist driven to madness by the souls of the characters he painted. She was disturbed by the film.

It was a winter of learning for Jean and her family. Gordon recommended books and she read them, improving her knowledge of literature, encouraging her to think in a more objective way. They played chess, although he was not a match for her. She had developed quite a strategic approach to the game. He doted on Alan. He assisted Jessie with her studies. David, the younger boy, was more interested in numbers than letters, taking delight in sharing difficult calculations:

"If three cats kill three mice in three minutes, how long does it take a hunner cats tae kill a hunner mice?" he'd ask.

"One hundred minutes," replied Gordon.

"No, no . . . it's still three minutes, ye daftie," said Jean, as David shared in her laughter.

"Weel, foo aboot 'is een, you two, David would continue, Which een o' ye'll be first to get the right answer: Imagine you are a banker and have £1000 and 10 envelopes. Foo would ye divide the money between the envelopes, sealing

them, and still be able to distribute, to a client, ony sum of
money between £1 and £1000, without opening any of the
envelopes?"

"I'll think about it, Davie," laughed Gordon, "although I
suspect your sister will beat me to it."

It took Jean several days to figure out the solution.
Gordon gave up.

One Sunday morning in May, Jean hired a pony and gig,
complete with driver. She thought that horse-drawn
transport would be quieter, less conspicuous. It was also
slightly cheaper. They set off for Whiteness as the first rays
of thin sunlight tried to warm the still cold voar earth.
Bobby, the driver, chatted cheerfully about trivia. She was
glad of his undemanding company. He dropped her by the
roadside in South Whiteness. The graveyard was quite close,
with a high wall around it. He agreed to collect her in an
hour.

She had no trouble finding the grave. It was the one with
an impressive new granite stone, still bedecked with a few
bunches of primroses, the mayflowers he had always loved.
She knelt and prayed. She spoke to him, telling him of Alan
and feeling his essence seeping into her being, easing her
heartache as morphine relieves pain. She was thankful that
she had come. She laid a single red paper rose on the stone.
She had purchased it, along with two dozen clothes pegs,
from the door-to-door tinker, Old Scratcher, a worthy who, as
the name implied, scratched herself constantly, irritated by
goodness knows what microscopic flora and fauna. Still, she
made elegant paper flowers and Willie would appreciate a
tinker's rose.

As she stood up, she came face to face with Billy Leask.
He was staring at her in bewilderment.

CHAPTER
28
Hope

"Jean, . . . Jean, is it dee? . . . What on earth is du doing here?"

"Eh . . . I . . . I came to pay my respects. He was . . . a friend o' mine."

"I didna ken dat . . . it's nice o' dee to come, Jean." Billy explained that he'd been checking his aunt Willa's sheep, it being lambing time, and he'd noticed a gig dropping somebody off.

". . . I didna even ken du wis back, Jean . . . dir's so much happened . . . I dinna ken what tae ask dee first." He was hopelessly embarrassed, she knew, not knowing where to begin. Like herself.

"I heard ye were wounded," she said at last, hearing the words as if they came from someone else.

"Yes. A'm much better noo though, A'm nearly aa dere . . ." He held up his right hand with its missing fingers . . . "I wis kinda scatterbrained fur a while . . . Oh, Jeanie, A'm blyde to see dee . . . du looks splendid."

She blushed at the compliment but felt truly ill at ease. Her pulse had quickened to an alarming rate and she was afraid that her voice shook, "I have to go noo," she said, " My hire will be waiting."

"Oh," he said, ". . . but I wid lik tae hae a spaek wi' dee . . . tae hear aboot dee family and . . . just tae fin oot hoo . . . Jeanie, I've thought o' dee a lot, du kens."

She wanted to run, to escape this tension that snagged her every thought and turned her throat to sandpaper.

"I'll walk back wi' dee, if dat's aright. Du can tell me de story." He smiled a familiar smile.

Falteringly, she told him how she had lost her husband and that she had a son and that she had nursed in Glasgow. She spoke of his father's kindness at the time James had been drowned. In turn, she heard the details of his accident and his recovery. He mentioned his business and his hopes for it. A more easy air started to develop between them.

The gig clopped into view and soon drew to a standstill

beside them.

"Cheerio, Billy. I'm glad things are working oot fur you."

"Can I see dee again, Jean?" he ventured.

"I..I dinna ken, Billy, maybe it's nae sic a . . ." Even as she spoke, she hoped that he would insist. She had no idea how she would explain Alan, how she could ever relate the past. He was Willie's flesh and blood, a half-brother to her own son . . . what a tangle of thought . . . her mind raced . . . she must stall for time: "I've a lot to occupy me at the moment . . . things are nae straighforward. I'm going oot wi' somebody. I would appreciate it if you didna come to see me . . ."

She climbed aboard.

He looked offended, she thought. The gig started to pull away. He walked alongside for a few yards.

"Alright, Jean, I'll leave it just noo if dat's what du wants. I'm busy eenoo onywye, between me business and havin tae tak ower Willa's croft . . . but tell me where tae find dee, and I'll look dee up when the lambing is feenished . . . just fur old time's sake."

She shouted the address and their eyes made contact. The years dropped away and there was a glint of hope. It was a communication bereft of innocence, scarred by experiences. Hope or maybe hopelessness.

29

Dark Secret

Billy was thrilled to meet her again, yet confused and a bit hurt by her apparent aloofness. Why was she so reluctant to see him? She had mentioned a suitor . . . who? She had been so dear to him as a teenager . . . but she was now a grown woman, a widow. Females . . . strange creatures, he would never understand them. Give me an engine any day, he thought.

He was tempted to ignore her words and knock on her door but he was too proud. He also feared rejection. Anyway, he was busy and work was a fine antidote for thwarted feelings. His engineering business was flourishing. He needed to engage more staff, he knew, because Michael and himself were overworked. The paperwork was especially demanding, now that every mechanically propelled vehicle used on a public road had to be registered and an excise licence obtained from the County Council. In addition, he had promised to oversee Willa's croft, the old soul being less and less able to cope.

A week later, he was walking on the hill savouring the crisp daylight and his solitude. It was always busy at lambing and by the time his tasks were complete, his heart had overcome his pride. He had made a decision. A morning call on Willa had helped, since, in the course of conversation, it transpired that Jean had been with a coachload of townsfolk on an outing and had almost given birth in her very hoose. That further explained the friendship with his father, who had been summoned to the emergency. However, Willa was under the impression that she had lost the baby. She must have been mistaken, because Jean definitely said she had a son. His aunt was getting a bit dottled, of course. She probably had a near miscarriage and his father saved the child. That explained it. Yes, she would have been through a lot of pain at that time, losing her husband so tragically. He would swallow his silly pride and call.

He skipped over the hill, his mind racing and his heart singing. Several of the ewes were hand tame, coming willingly to his side in search of titbits. Like Willa, he often carried a handful of stale bread or vegetable parings in his pocket for his favourites. He spoke to the grey one with the black face and the doleful eyes as she nuzzled to his side without fear, confident in this new shepherd that had replaced the old one. He cupped his hand over the soft nose as the eager wet tongue licked his fingers in expectation.

"Sorry, lass, nothin fur dee da day . . . but will du wish me luck? I've made me mind up, I'm going tae see her da night. She seemed dat distant, du sees . . . and dir's been dat much water under da bridge . . . I winder whit'll becum o' wis. Oh that my life wir as simple as dine, enough tae aet and a decent bit o' shalter ahint da dykes . . . and du's happy . . . But I want . . . dat much mair dan dat!"

The zinc bath soaked off the engine grease. Then he sleeked his hair and donned his better clothes. Staring at the mirror, he noted that he had broadened. He was a young man, barely twenty-three, but the anxieties of the years had already aged him. He had earned the stress lines and shadows around his eyes.

Whistling, he spat on his shoes and polished them into a shine, before putting on his jacket and brushing the fluffs off the collar. He was nervous. It had been a long time, and no doubt she had other far more piquant memories than a fleeting childhood romance of long ago. He hurried to his car and drove to Lerwick.

Meanwhile, Jean, grieving for Willie, pondered this strange emotional triangle. Was it possible? . . . Unusual, but yes, perfectly possible. Attraction to a second did not necessarily lessen the bond with the first. She loved her mother no less when her brother was around. If she had a second child, it could not change her love for Alan. Willie would have understood her logic. Yet, it did not seem right. Was it wrong? Would Billy, or anyone else for that matter, accept such a strange situation?

There was a knock on the door. Flustered, she stammered some apology about not expecting anyone. Surely he must be aware of how her heart leapt. In awkward silence, Billy shuffled on the threshold.

"We..el, aye, come awa in . . . I'm sorry."

She made a panicky inventory of defects in her appearance and the state of the house, magnifying every tiny imperfection and wished that she'd been alerted of his coming. At least Alan was still out with Elsie.

"Would ye like some tea?"

Billy laughed, "Yes please Jean. I just thought I'd come and spaek tae dee if du's no too busy?"

She brought tea and he began to talk. He was like his father, easy to listen to, quick to put her at ease. He told about his missing years and the sad satisfaction of the final months with Willie. Her eyes moistened with the pity of stolen time.

"Billy, there is something afa important that I maun tell ye," she said suddenly and firmly. " It is a personal matter, difficult to talk aboot . . . It concerns my past . . . and my son." She fought to find the right words to express raw truth.

"Jeanie, if it's something fae da past, hit dusna really matter."

"It's about m' loonie. My husband was nae Alan's father."

Billy extended a finger to touch her lips, "Shh, Jeanie. I dinna need tae ken aboot it . . . Just answer me one thing, is the bairn's faider still involved in dee life?"

"He's deed, Billy. I loved him dearly and I will never forget him."

"Then I dinna hiv tae ken, Jeanie. He must've been a good man to hiv deserved dee. We must not dwell on da past, lass. If dir's one thing dat da war's taught me, hit's appreciation of freends and family . . . even da everyday peerie things that I used to tak for granted . . . lik dis cup o' tae. I even appreciate me midder mair, A'm inclined tae mak allooances . . . and I want tae settle doon wi' a family o' me ain noo."

I've thought aboot dee a lok ower da years, Jean, and noo A'm askin dee tae gie me some hope. I ken we're baith older and wiser, but we did feel a love fur een anither wance. I tink it could still be dere."

The moment of truth, she thought, her head bent. Then the moment was broken as the door burst inward and Elsie entered, with the bairn and a bucket of partans. She put the child down on his feet, where he stood clinging to her skirt, before dropping to his knees and scuttling gleefully across the floor to his mother, ignoring the stranger. Radiant with pleasure, he indicated the pail:

"Ook, mama . . . cwabs..see dem."

"I see them, sweetheart, they're lovely!"

She did the introductions and Alan now appraised their visitor with open curiosity. Billy stared at him.

There was an awkward silence. He stared at Jean, then back at the cute little cherub with the dimple, then back at Jean. It was like looking at a swaddling photograph of himself in the cot! The reluctant thought dazed his mind. God Almighty . . . He turned to her with wide questioning eyes.

She met his gaze unflinching. "Aye," she said, "he's yer brither."

"Oh, Jeanie!" he said. He uttered a few token words to her grandmother, then got up and politely wished them goodnight.

He searched frantically through his father's personal effects, knowing that Agnes would have had no interest in them. He read through the notebook and he fixed on one of his last poems. Only then did he accept the truth without a shadow of doubt.

His sympathy for his mother was intense . . . She had been cruelly wronged . . . Did she know? No wonder she'd been so difficult to live with if that's the way he'd behaved . . . throughout their married lives maybe. He would spend time with her, make amends. As for Jean, she was no better than...at least the whore Michelle was honest and straightforward . . . Jean, well . . . wasn't she a Scottie fishwife, the bitch. His mother had been right.

He went out into the night, banging the door, abuse screaming in his head. Bitter with hurt, angry and miserable, typically human.

CHAPTER
30
Springtime

The weeks faded into months and Jean did not see Billy again. She gave up hope. She tried to put him out of her mind, but he persistently niggled away at her weak moments, especially when she was alone at night, or in her dreams. She still saw Gordon occasionally, although she had discovered that there were several other long-standing adoring women in his life. She felt relieved. She threw herself into the lives of her family, spending time with her sister Jessie and with her mother, realising that they both had hidden depths of intellect that she had barely noticed before. "It's funny. We get so tied up in our petty lives that we do not appreciate treasures on our own doorstep!" she said to Alan, who gurgled in agreement.

He was growing fast. Mary, who was in much better health although the remnants of the racking cough never left her, looked after him sometimes and thrived in the grandmother role. She had fewer demands on her time these days, very different from the old frantic chores of line baiting and net mending that used to dominate life when her own children were little.

Elsie, now in her late seventies, surprised the whole family by announcing that she was "going to wed". The lucky gentleman, for such he had become, was Teenie's Black Jock! He was nowadays as pink and sweet and shaven as a baby. He had bought and renovated a gutters' hut at Gremista and had wooed the old lady until he won the pledge. She had kept him at arm's length until his metamorphosis from midden to man was complete. She had also waited until Mary and the grandchildren needed her less.

"He's nae a saint, Jeanie, but he's a good man and he'll be good company for my auld age, . . . when it comes, that is!" Elsie chuckled.

Once the initial shock had subsided, everybody wished her all the best. After a quiet wedding, her health was drunk. Teenie's Black Jock celebrated more fully than anyone else, then promised not to do it again. Elsie moved out of

Klondyke Cottages. Johnie rented a place of his own in preparation for marriage, leaving only the youngest two, David and Jessie. Jean longed for a place of her own as well, but soon discovered that a single woman with a fatherless child was not classed as a good tenant. Furthermore, money was tight, her part-time jobs barely covering her living expenses.

The fishing had not recaptured its pre-war success. Johnie had to work even harder to maintain earnings as the price of herring was falling year by year . . . £2 5s a cran in 1919, £1 1s 2d in 1920, and now down to £1 0s 7d. There was also a scarcity of fuel due to a national coal strike. As it continued, even the larger boats, lying idle in southern ports, were forced to lay off young seamen, who returned to Shetland with every steamer. Whaling was also in decline, due to adverse publicity and a consequent drop in the market for whale oil. A decision was made to close the Olna and Collafirth stations causing much hardship in Delting and Northmavine as men lost vital jobs.

Unemployment and poor wages predisposed to low morale among the fisherfolk and disputes with the town authorities broke out easily. Several of the seafood stalls at Alexandra Wharf were closed down by the sanitary inspector and damning letters were published about diseases harboured by body vermin, especially in some classes of worker serving the public. Various proposals were put forward for the acute sore throat epidemic that swept the town, including the usual "soothmoother" origin. However, the quality of the town gas was eventually blamed for this particular problem!

It was not surprising that many of the Scotties and their children, including Johnie and David were questioned by the police following a serious fire at the Unemployment Bureau in North Roadside. All records were totally destroyed. There was a chequered history to the wooden building, which had started life as a naval recreation hut, erected by the Church Army on Alexandra Wharf, in 1918. It was dismantled and moved, in 1920, by the Seamen's Mission (R.N.M.D.S.F.) and served for a while as a clubroom for resident fishermen, before being taken over by the Labour Bureau. The police were unable to prove arson, although suspicions were strong and the incident did nothing to ease the conflict with the Scotties.

Despite the recession, some seafaring progress was evident such as the grand opening of the Malakoff dry-dock facility. Johnie and Jean attended the ceremony where the steam drifter Sumburgh Head was levered out of the water by Mrs. J. D. Ganson amidst three cheers from the crowd. Cake and wine were provided for a select few dignitaries. Yet, there were few such reasons to celebrate. In an attempt to help people cope with their difficulties, the Mission encouraged public meetings. Jean attended the rivetting address by Mr. Andrew Cowe, entitled "Strive."

She did strive, but she was lonely, especially in her bed at night. Having tasted true love, with its tantalising blend of friendship and desire, she knew that she was not cut out to be celibate. There has to be more to life than this mundane day to day existence, she thought. She needed a fresh start at life, a new opportunity.

She scanned the situations vacant column in the Shetland Times looking for a better position. She seriously considered emigration. The advertisement was tempting:-

"Experienced domestic servants wanted for New Zealand.

Free passage + £2 expenses on joining steamer. Parties of girls accompanied by Matron, London to New Zealand. Received on arrival by Women Government Officials. Reliable situations guaranteed. Excellent climate, Good wages.

Write to:- High Commissioner for New Zealand. Emigration Sector 415, Strand, London."

She wrote. A curt reply said that they were not looking for unmarried mothers.

Johnie and his fiancé set their wedding date for the beginning of August. There was great excitement as the time approached. As a practical and inexpensive marriage gift, Jean asked if she could decorate their rooms. She did not mind the labour involved and, besides, she had developed an aesthetic eye for making places look clean and attractive on little outlay.

She purchased whitewash for the walls and a new piece of waxed floorcloth, with a splattered pattern, a perfect disguise for a busy, or less than perfect, housewife!

Gordon, who appeared periodically when he was short of female company, offered to lend a hand. A week before the big day he was busy with a whitewash brush on a kitchen wall, while she scrubbed the skirting boards ready for varnishing. They finished by mid-evening and sat down for a well earned cup of tea, contented that the task was complete and oblivious to the freckle-splotches on their hands, faces and hair. The place looked bright and warming and the smell of paint was intoxicating. Outside it was summer and the heady scent of lush garden growth came in through the open window of the little flat, depositing an essence of vigour and strength. Alan lay asleep in the bedroom. Jean went to refill the cups.

"There's somebody at the door, Jeanie, Shall I get it?" Gordon called to her.

"Oh, aye please, Gordon, but . . . I'm nae expecting onybody. Johnie's boat is aff the night."

She recognised the voice and felt faint. She heard him usher the visitor in.

"Hello, Jean, . . . I wis just passing. I thought I'd look in and see hoo . . . I hope I'm no interruptin onything!"

It was clear that he was drunk. He smiled sarcastically at them and she had an uncomfortable feeling that he saw her confusion and was mocking her. She introduced him. He did not shake hands, but sneered and said:

"Anidder wan o' dee conquests, nae doobt!" Turning to Gordon, he added: " Hoo does it feel tae hae her fur a concubine, then?"

"I believe that is entirely unjustified, Mr. Leask. Jean and I are good friends, that is all," Gordon responded.

"Dat'll be right. I'm heard aa dat afore . . ." Billy shouted, as bitterness and jealousy spilled over in his alcohol-numbed brain. An angry fist crunched into Gordon's nose. Billy staggered to a chair and sat, head in hands, meek after his impulsive outburst. Jean seethed with rage and embarrassment and brought a towel to soak up the blood.

"This kind of behaviour cannot be tolerated, Jean," mumbled Gordon, " I fully intend to report this incident. This fellow needs a lesson in manners. He certainly owes us both an apology."

"Oh, Gordon, dinna be silly . . . he's drunk," she said.

"All the more reason," Gordon replied, " I'll go now. I trust you'll be all right?"

"She'll be aa right . . . A'm goin onywye . . . dinna ken why I cam in da first place.."

Billy rose and fumbled his way out the door. Nevertheless, an assault and a disturbance of the peace was reported to the police. After that, Jean did not see Gordon for several days. Then he called to inform her that he was betrothed to marry one of his teaching colleagues. Jean wished him well. She would miss his company but was glad that he had found a partner. She was relieved to hear that Billy Leask had got off with a warning and would not be charged.

Jean took Alan to the Fish Trade Gala Day in the Gilbertson Park. He enjoyed the excitement, especially when he was allowed to toddle in the egg and spoon race. Billy made a sporadic appearance among the crowd . . . obviously drunk. He did not speak to them, but followed them around for a while. She understood his inward conflict and waited, hopeful. He got into a grand car and drove away. Later, in the Shetland Times, she read of the collision:

"A sentence of fourteen days imprisonment was passed at the Mansion House on August 20th, for drunkeness. Mr. Richard Tudor Edwards, surgeon, certified the defendant, William Leask, drunk. He was fined 20/- with £2 5/- costs for driving to the common danger and his licence has been revoked."

Life in Lerwick resumed an element of its previous, humdrum, cosmopolitan style. The Dutch fleet were back for yet another summer (Marie Henriette; Gesina; Flevo IV); the Swedish line fishing smacks arrived again at Baltasound; steam whalers berthed at Olnafirth from Grangemouth (Swona; Sacra; Solva; Spuma), only to be disappointed; and, as if there had never been a war, German vessels were prominent in the harbour (Brook; Kartreprel; Bellwarder; Wandrahn; Max Schmidt). It's funny how some things in life change so fast, while others never seem to change at all, Jean thought.

She saw little of Billy. Rumour had it that he was drinking heavily and his business was suffering. He was also said to frequent the company of prostitutes. She began to wonder why she had ever been attracted to him. He was not like his father at all. He was a cold, hard engineer. But why could she not rid herself of this caring? Why did he yet fill her thoughts?

In March, 1922, she saw the death notice of . . . *Agnes Leask, beloved wife of the late Dr. William Leask.* She had never liked the woman, but for the sake of courtesy, she wrote a letter:

"Dear Billy,
I want to let you know that I am sorry about your mother.

166

I lack ability to express my thoughts and emotions. I cannot truthfully explain my past actions. I think we must all be honest with ourselves and answer to our own consciences. I have no regrets about my child. If you expect an apology, I cannot give you that.

However, I do care about you. My thoughts are with you now. Whatever the future holds, I wish you well.
Jean."

There is something about the loss of a parent that causes people to stop and think fundamentally, as if the death bed has transferred its urgency to the living, imploring them to resolutions. He read between the lines of Jean's letter and resolved to count his blessings and to forgive. He would stop the boozing, devote himself to his business, and, if she would have him, take her back into his life, slowly and carefully. He suddenly knew that his casual women meant nothing. They eased a temporary pain, like Michelle, that was all.

A whole year had passed since he had seen her at his father's grave and first thought of asking if she'd like to come to Whiteness and see the lambs on Willa's croft. She was wary, but she came.

It was mid-May. The mayflowers were in bloom on every hillside and in every ditch. Marsh marigolds, ragged robin, ladysmock and orchids were beginning to blossom, although the yellow heads of the stately flag irises were not yet peeping through their green sheaths. The wild flowers were a welcome sight signifying a rebirth of an old perennial life, while the romping lambs, by their mother's sides, symbolised a new generation. The pure white of the lambs contrasted starkly with the weather-beaten fawn of the tattered ewes. As Jean looked at their innocent exuberant frolics, racing each other, leaping for joy, playing king of the castle on every crag, somersaulting a ewe's back, she felt a bond with the whole regenerative process of nature.

"Fit's the matter wi' 'at one? Is it lost?" she said, pointing and hurrying to a corner of the park.

A weak, sunken sided, skeletal loner stood shivering there, ears drooping and back hunched. Jean felt a surge of maternal instinct.

"Weel, hit's no very happy wi' itsel, dat's fur sure. Hit could be ill . . . or lost . . . maybe hit's wan o' da twins 'at wis born yisterday. Pick hit up and we'll hae a look aroond fur da yowe."

167

She cradled the scrap of wool and bone. It did not resist, but emitted a plaintive bleating sound, which continued periodically as she carried it in her jacket. They crossed a hill, towards the west banks. Some distance down the steep slope on the other side, they heard the acknowledging call of an old ewe. She came slowly to investigate, a single lamb trailing behind her. She was clearly the mother of the ailing creature. She was very thin and she limped badly, holding one foreleg in the air.

"Footrot!" Billy said, "She's no able fur twa o' dem. Yun een likely followed anidder yowe last night. I'll trim her feet."

He upturned the animal and skilfully whittled away the rotted hoof, which looked like a massive ingrowing toe-nail. It smelt terrible and bled as he pared it to the healthy tissue. As he worked with the ewe, balanced on its rump, Jean held the undernourished lamb to the udder. It suckled eagerly, tail wagging, happy, slaked from thirst. She smiled with satisfaction.

"I'll caa da three o' dem intae da yard later on, just tae keep an eye on dem. The auld yowe dusna hae much milk for two really."

They continued down to the shore of Stromness Voe. Gulls were gossiping overhead and tirricks on the small offshore holm were holding a frantic conference about the human intruders approaching their territory. A few bold birds swooped on the strangers as they passed on by, heading South towards the point and the open sea. The mouth of the voe was narrow, and Jacksville House, on Binna Ness, stood tall like an impressive gatehouse, guarding the entrance. The imposing architecture of such a castle-like edifice was strangely out of character for Shetland, she thought. There were only two crofthouses on the far shore, the nearest called Cogtoon, where Billy waved to a man with a collie. On the several miles of coastline, there was only one other solitary house, Pund, nestling in a little cove, a beautifully sheltered spot with its own little beach and slipway.

Piles of driftwood were laid up on the grassy banks, claimed but not yet collected. A grey seal popped his head out of the water only yards from the shore and stared at the two of them with brown wide-eyed melancholy. It seemed to be asking mute imponderable questions from its watery haven.

"It's aa right, we winna touch dee, boy." Billy shouted. It submerged in distrust.

"Foo div ye ken it's a loon?"

168

"Weel, A'm no sure, but dere.." Billy pointed to a different movement in the water. "Dat's certainly a girl!"

An otter with two kits was swimming just offshore. She lay on her back and made an angry "chit . . . chit . . . chit . . ." noise, protecting her young, livid at the human animals, sensing their awesome and dreadful power, yet emboldened with universal maternal instinct. Jean laughed. This place was full of beauty and wonder, so different from the life she had always known.

They stopped beside a dry stone dyke and, unwittingly, he stumbled on a moss-capped boulder and brushed against her arm. Achingly aware of his touch, she ran her fingers over the ancient lichened stones imagining the hands that put them there. She sensed the joy of life in the wall, but there was also sorrow there. Life was like that. She felt his eyes on her, pinning her to the wall, questioning.

"Billy, div you remember, years ago, saying ye'd tak me tae see a real holm in Whiteness someday?"

"I mind it weel, Jeanie, and I havna forgotten, but my peerie boat is no i' da water yet, the weather hasna been settled, but I'm thinking tae launch her shortly. We'll tak a trip the next fine weekend. Noo, I think we'll turn for hame, it's a good hour tae Hallibrig and hit'll be dark by den."

He stopped to investigate a sheep alone on the rocky shore. She was keeping faithful vigil over a dead lamb, it's eyes and tongue already pecked out by blackback gulls. Saying nothing, but with a downcast face, he took a piece of string from his pocket, tied it around the hind leg of the carcass, and fed out a length. Then they walked on, Billy trailing the limp body behind him. There was something distasteful and undignified about the flapping and thumping motion as the lamb bounced along, but there was method in this madness. The ewe followed demurely behind, her nose to the smell of her baby, bleating to it all the while in tones of endearment and concern, oblivious to death.

"Fit'll ye do wi' her?"

"Dis'll solve da problem o' yun yowe wi twins. A'll leave da poorly een wi' hit's ain midder and gie da healthier twin tae dis yowe. A'll hae tae skin dis een and pit da skin on to da foster lamb. Dis yowe's a good midder, she'll accept it nae bother . . . it's a messy procedure, though, but sometimes it has to be done. You hiv tae be cruel tae be kind."

She watched the operation with interest. She could see that this apparently hard and callous act was necessary to achieve a just and caring aim. She had a lot to learn.

She was beginning to understand the way of the land. It was very different from the way of the sea.

31
Integration

Jean was on duty at the sanatorium when two patients with suspected scarlet fever were brought in from the Dutch Mission ship "De Hoop." Shortly afterwards, Alan became ill. Jean would not leave his side. She nursed the bright red, blotchy, vomiting, child. Billy admired her dedication. Although he had resented Alan initially, he was a winning youngster, intelligent, sweet, innocent, tottering around with endless curiosity at the wonder of his world. After the hurt of the child's very existence, Billy had mellowed with time. He could not help being drawn to the little fellow. He willed him to get better, not just for Jean's sake, but because he himself now cared. Then, just as Alan recovered, Jean herself contracted the disease.

It was a particularly virulent outbreak and she became very ill, with a raging fever. She was unable to eat. Jessie nursed her, sponging her body several times a day to reduce temperature and forcing her to drink fluids. At the end of a fortnight, she was still emaciated with sickness, near comatose, and they feared she might die. It was a critical time. The anxiety focussed Billy's mind powerfully. It put the past into perspective, the mortality of man, the certainty of death, the variable sweetness of life. The thin drizzle of his recent existence seemed meaningless. Why had he wasted precious time on what now seemed like trivia.

He was not afraid of the fever. He came every day, solemn and sober, speaking gentle words by her side, helping to turn her to prevent bed sores. He stroked her damp hair and liked to touch the fine bone structure of her face and shoulders.

Alan latched on to him during his visits. He spent time with the boy, who was almost back to full health yet too young to understand the gravity of his mother's condition. In the early evenings, to give the family a chance to wash and change the patient, he would often walk the boy along the length of Lerwick harbour, Alan running ahead, pointing out the landmarks familiar to him . . . uncle Johnie's boat . . . each species of fish he saw in the quayside boxes:

" 'At ones is flooks, Biwly! . . . and 'at ones is skate, . . . and 'at ones is tuk (tusk.) "

Billy caught him in his arms and hugged this little bundle of convalescing energy, touching the hollow of the dimple on his chin and reciting:

"On the baby's knuckle . . . or the baby's knee . . . where will the baby's dimple be . . ." but trailing off as he could not maintain the forced attempt to be cheerful. He squeezed the child very hard, willing Jeanie better, praying for the first time in years.

One evening, when they got back to Klondyke cottages, she looked stronger. She had been bathed as usual and her hair was combed. She wore a fresh white cotton night-gown and the air smelt of methylated spirit. It had been Billy himself who had suggested dabbing a little meths on her, because it evaporated quickly and took heat away with it. It also toughened the damp skin that lay in contact with the bedclothes. She seemed to be sleeping more peacefully than of late and her pallid cheeks now had a touch of colour, like rouge circles on a china doll. He took her thin, translucent hand in his, cradling her leaden arm. He said:

"Jeanie, I'm sorry I judged dee, lass, I've nae right tae do dat. Dinna gie up on me noo, Jeanie . . . I luv dee."

She whimpered and her eyelids flickered. He thought he caught the hint of a smile and, some minutes later, he felt her fingers tighten on his rough engineer's hands.

Jessie came into the room just then: "The doctor's been today, Billy. He thinks her fever's broken. She's past the worst, but very weak. It's up to us now."

There followed a steady improvement, a time of hope and building. However, it was many weeks before she was well enough for the long promised trip.

―――――――

They launched the boat at the Nesbister beach, rowing out past the various small islets: Hoove Holm, Otter Holm and Cure Holm. They passed the forsaken old fishing station, the Böd of Nesbister.

They continued out beyond Kirk Skerry as far as Burwick Holm, savouring their time together, a restrained time, full of unspoken confessions, tingling with telepathic awareness. They wanted to make the day last, fearful that the anticipation was sweeter than whatever else might come. There was an atmosphere of softly seductive tension,

172

seasoned with uncertainty. There was a promise of contentment, yet a small niggling fear of rejection. Near the neck of the voe, the swell from the open sea was much stronger and they turned back. As they approached Otter Holm, seals that were sunning themselves on the crags slithered their clumsy blubbery retreat into the sea and became instantly graceful.

They pulled the prow of the little boat out of the water and secured her. The holm itself was grassy on top of jagged black rocks and reminded Jean of the Sands of Sound all those years ago. The last few stragglers of a new generation of fledgling birds scurried in the grass to the white splattered shore, pretending to be invisible. Forlorn remnants of speckled eggshells lay here and there.

The evidence of an otter habitat was everywhere. The overgrown vegetation was riddled with tunnels so that walking was difficult and the distinctive musky smell was sharp on the air. A solitary otter popped a head out of a burrow and made a hissing noise before diving into the sea. Several other heads appeared on the surface of the water, whiskered, curious, flat faces, submerging again quickly, shy, but not threatening. Their young were well raised, maternal instinct now diluted.

The powdery withering heads of sea pinks adorned the overhangs. They found a sheltered secluded spot, looking out towards the islands of Langa, Papa and West Burra and to the distant cliffs of Fitful Head. Here, the tall grasses stood shoulder high. They were cocooned in a pocket of pure nature, cut off from the world by a moat of sea, a place where the meeting of land and sea was condensed.

"It's beautiful, Billy. I'm so glad to be alive..and there's nowhere I'd rather be than here."

"Du's beautiful, Jeanie. A'm glad du's alive and here . . . wi' me."

They had both come home, seeking asylum. She put her head on his shoulder and he put his arms around her and drew her close. She was warm and pliable. The avalanche of pent-up feelings came then, a great symphony of emotions; anger, regret, tenderness, urgency. The poetry of love was theirs.

The universe was reduced to this tiny holm and soon became concentrated in an even smaller and more sacred space, where maybe they glimpsed the secret of life itself as their cry of exaltation rang out with the wild things across

173

Whiteness Voe. Spoken pledges of lifelong commitment were not necessary. They both knew and understood.

After observing the two minutes of silence, they were married on November 11, 1922, and the celebration of Armistice day seemed doubly meaningful.

On November 25th, following a longstanding campaign by the fishermen to improve safety at sea, Captain Drury, Inspector of Lifeboat Stations visited the islands aboard St. Rognvald. He held several meetings throughout the community but no definite promise of a lifeboat was made.

On November 29th, the Prosperity went down in hurricane force winds, five miles north east of Bressay. All hands were lost. The bodies were never recovered.

Eight-year-old John Watt Leask went everywhere with his brother Alan. Despite nearly three years' difference in their ages, they were often mistaken for twins. They looked alike. Each had a dimple on his chin, both were full of mischief, with fun-loving warm temperaments. They lived in a renovated old crofthouse on the knowe at Hallibrig, a happy place where an auntie called Willa had once lived. They were enrolled in the Whiteness school and well integrated into the community.

Alan was busy making plans to spend his first summer aboard his uncle David's boat. He was daft on the fishing, taking a keen interest in modern developments, like the seine net (introduced in 1926, but making an impact only in the 1940's). He was already a fairly competent marine engineer. John liked nothing better than to help his father with the croft, especially the lambing and the shearing. He wrote poetry, like his grandfather. Both of them liked to have oily dirty hands as they tinkered with machinery in their father's workshop.

The oil, the water, the land and the blood had mixed.

Integration was beginning.

Epilogue

A new population of incomers now mingles with the indigenous people of Lerwick and encounters the prejudices of our town. The hybrid youth think that they alone have problems of integration, that only they are familiar with the haunts of Lerwick, the streets and closes that have bred so many generations.

There is still a reaction to soothmoothers: English, German, Chinese, Indian, Pakistani, South African, . . . the list is endless, although it is notable that these modern migrants have mostly come into positions of authority or into a flourishing private business sector. Consequently, they are able to demand more respect than the poverty stricken fisherfolk who struggled to survive under more powerful bias at the turn of the century.

However, it is interesting now to consider the fate of the sons, daughters, grandchildren and great grandchildren of the Scottie migrants. They are now well mixed, indistinguishable from the native Shetlanders (an ill-defined term, since the natives themselves are descendants of many previous migrants: Picts, Vikings, Icelanders, Faroese, . . .) The hallmark of these integrated Scotties remains their surname (Watt, Wiseman, West, . . .) They have intermarried and the hybrid vigour is evident in every sector of our community.

Fishing remains the single most important primary industry in Shetland in 1994. Aided by diversification into salmon farming, it has survived the oil era. There is little doubt that the Scottie migrants influenced its development and success, with their determination and expertise. Seining was introduced to Shetland in the second and third decade of the century, the process being much influenced by the trials and experiences of the Scottie fishermen. It is notable that the coxswain of the first Lerwick Lifeboat in 1930 was John

Watt (not the fictitious character appearing in this volume) and the "Lady Jane and Martha Ryland", in her first twelve months at sea, saved the lives of thirty-four men.

Without the successive influxes of soothmoothers, the coefficient of inbreeding in parts of Shetland would mitigate against our present enviable state of genetic health and it is likely that the mean pupil performance in our outstanding schools would be poorer. We have much to thank soothmoothers for. The determined will integrate.

Glossary

This list is intended as a brief guide to a few words and phrases used throughout the text. The reader is further referred to "The Shetland Dictionary, by John J. Graham" for a more precise coverage of the Shetlandic.

almark yowe: a sheep that jumps over or breaks
     through fences.
baal awa: throw away.
bawbee: halfpenny.
beilin: septic and throbbing.
bide: stay.
bile: boil.
blyde: glad.
breeks: trousers.
brönnie: a round, thick oatmeal scone.
caa canny: be careful.
caerd: card.
chaff-seck: chaff filled mattress.
cloots: cloths or bandages wrapped around gutter's fingers.
clertit: besmeared.
dab hand: expert.
deen: done.
dere: there ("th" is often replaced by "d" in Shetlandic.)
dirl: reverberate.
div: do.
doad: dollop.
dock: backside.
döless: lacking in energy.
dottled: in dotage.
dritten-lik: look of disappointment on face,
     following reprimand.
dunter: eider duck.
ettercap: a spider-like person with a venomous nature.
fan: found.
fantin: starving.
far: where.
feart: afraid.
flayed: skinned.
florin: two shilling coin.

flytin: scolding.
foo: how.
furt: out-of-doors.
futret: ferret or weasel.
gansey: jersey.
glansin: sparkling.
gyaets: paths.
gypper: knife.
haaf: deep sea beyond coastal waters.
had yer wheest: be quiet.
hale: whole.
henkel-trams: shaky on the legs.
hoostak sloo: a big, fat, lazy person.
holm: small uninhabited island.
ive noo: just now.
langsome: lazy.
laverick: lark.
lipper: a nasty, unpleasant person.
little wirt: poorly.
loon (or loonie): boy.
manna: must not.
nark: annoy.
neeps: turnips.
new-slippet: just released, after being confined.
nev-foo: handful.
nowt: cattle.
orra: rough.
peer: poor.
peerie: small.
pewl: seagull.
puckle: few.
quine (or quinie): girl.
redd oot: untangle and clear of debris.
roozer: watering can.
riggs: fields.
rivlins: simple hide shoes.
sharny: covered in dung.
sherger: nagger.
sic: such.
skirl: cry.
smoorikin: kiss.
sna-greemet: a thin cover of snow, dark patches showing.
sooked piltock: lightly salted and dried young saithe.
steeped: soaked.
syne: then.
thole: endure.
thrawn: obstinate.
tippins: ends of lines with hooks attached.
traughle: struggle.
trumsket: sulky, unsociable.
voar: Spring.
wupped: bound.